Praise for *Blackwood*

.... captiv...... .... a sturdy Faulknerian theme – past and present are never exactly separated, and actions in the present are provoked by words or deeds from long ago. Michael Farris Smith's prose is calm yet full of feeling for this place and these people, and he handles scenes of introspection and scenes of hostility with equal skill. In Smith's hands, pages keep turning' – **Daniel Woodrell, *New York Times* bestselling author of *Winter's Bone***

'In Smith's haunting, engrossing latest (after *The Fighter*), strangers awaken an evil force lurking... Smith's meditation on the darkness of the human heart offers a moving update to the Southern gothic tradition' – ***Publishers Weekly***

'Lurking over *Blackwood* is a family of itinerant grifters – a version of Faulkner's Snopes clan, forces of chaos, human kudzu except for the youngest of them, a mysterious boy in whom Colburn sees his young self. As in the best noir, a soul-strangling inevitability hangs over Red Bluff, yet somehow Smith gives his doomed characters a dignity in the face of forces well beyond their control' – ***Booklist* (starred review)**

'Unsettling, heartbreaking, and frequently astonishing, this Southern gothic never runs out of revelations... A gleaming, dark masterpiece by one of Southern fiction's leading voices' – ***Kirkus* (starred review)**

'Call it Southern Noir or Southern Gothic or the legacy of Larry Brown but the reality is Michael Farris Smith is writing with one of the most powerful and distinctive voices in current fiction' – **Square Books**

Praise for *The Fighter*

'Like living language, literary modes have both a formal and a demotic form. What we call "noir" is high tragedy brought down to the forgotten and disavowed – the fallen, who can do little but go on falling. Ours to witness the beauty and power of their fall. With *The Fighter*, cleaving to tradition, Michael Farris Smith brings that tradition brilliantly into the present' – **James Sallis**

'Smith's fiction is full of hard people in tough situations, but his obvious love of language and innately rhythmic prose lift his stories to a higher level' *–Big Issue*

'Equal parts brutal and beautiful and harrowing, it's left me totally bereft' – **Chris Whitaker, author of *Tall Oaks* and *All The Wicked Girls***

'Crisply written tale of thwarted lives and raw-boned courage' – ***Booklist***

'This resourceful writer weds violence, despair, and glimmers of hope during a few tense days in the life of a once-legendary bareknuckle fighter... A gifted storyteller who parses battered dreams and the legacies of abandonment with a harsh realism that is both saddening and engaging' – *Kirkus* **(starred review)**

'Smith's great talent here is writing about ancient, universal concerns – parents and children, aging, and place – in a setting so vivid and specific that the book practically tracks mud up onto your doorstep. His vision of the Delta is powerful and lingering' – *New York Journal of Books*

'A novel that takes hold of your heart in a tight vice, *The Fighter*... is also written with diamond-like care and has a visceral impact, although not always for the faint-hearted' – *Crime Time*

'Smith's narrative manages to stay just ahead of disintegration, and does so with style, lush prose, and storytelling assurance... *The Fighter* is a triumph. It confirms Smith's status as one of our foremost authors in the Rough South, Grit Lit tradition established by Crews, Larry Brown, Tom Franklin, William Gay and the towering Cormac McCarthy' – *Clarion Ledger*

'*The Fighter* is a poetic and often dark look at the American South. Smith takes readers deep into the physical and spiritual heart of the landscape, building inexorably to a brutal, no-holds-barred finale' – *The Newton Review of Books*

'The characters Michael Farris Smith brings to life might have been found in the works of Emile Zola, flawed beings with a single-mindedness which makes them exceptional' – *Crime Review*

'Michael Farris Smith is continuing the southern gothic tradition of William Gay and Flannery O'Connor. Drenched in sorrow and written with complex language, *The Fighter* moves toward a conclusion both surprising and inevitable' – **Chris Offutt**

'One of those wonderful and rare books that's both a page turner and a novel of great depth and emotion. *The Fighter* is Southern Noir at its finest' – **Ace Atkins**

'*The Fighter* is a book I wish I'd written but am deeply grateful I got to read. It is a masterful portrait of place and character and how one influences the other, with language that is both brutal and tender at once' – **Attica Locke**

Praise for *Desperation Road*

'You will not be disappointed' – *Daily Mail*

'A wonderfully evoked and deeply touching work' – *Big Issue*

'Michael Farris Smith's prose focuses on small details and has a rhythm that gives it a poetic quality; a comparison with Annie Proulx is not overly enthusiastic' – *Crime Review*

'A brilliantly compelling novel' – **Robert Olen Butler**

'A harsh but beautiful thriller that has you cheering under your breath for its wounded, fallible protagonist throughout'
– *LoveReading*

'This is just stunning… little short of perfection… think Daniel Woodrell, Bill Beverly and Lou Berney for starters and that will give you an idea of the style, the range and the humanity of the novel' – **Graham Minett, author of *The Hidden Legacy***

'Smith handles agony with a devastating tenderness… in a selfish, predatory world, *Desperation Road* carves out a bloody chunk of redemption' – *Crime Scene*

'Cinema written all over it… a particularly good novel if you like whispering "Sh*t…" in an incredulous voice' – *Shortlist*

'An outstanding performance' – **Ron Rash**

Also by MICHAEL FARRIS SMITH

The Hands of Strangers

Rivers

Desperation Road

The Fighter

BLACKWOOD

MICHAEL FARRIS SMITH

NO EXIT PRESS

First published in the UK in 2020 by No Exit Press,
an imprint of Oldcastle Books Ltd,
Harpenden, UK
noexit.co.uk

A CIP catalogue record for this book is available from the British Library.

ISBN
978-0-85730-390-5 (Demy)
978-0-85730-391-2 (epub)

2 4 6 8 10 9 7 5 3 1

Typeset in 12.5pt Garamond MT
by Avocet Typeset, Bideford, Devon, EX39 2BP
Printed and bound in Great Britain by TJ International, Padstow, Cornwall

For more information about Crime Fiction go to @crimetimeuk

For Ellen

Foxes have dens and birds have nests,
  but the Son of Man has no place to lay his head.
                              — Matthew 8:20

1956

1

COLBURN WAS STANDING WITH HIS mother in the kitchen when she said go fetch your father. The long light of an August day bleeding through the windows. His face and hands dirty from playing football in the neighbor's yard. His mother wiped the sweat from his face with a dishtowel. Held his chin in her hand and gazed at him. You'll be twelve soon. I can't believe it. He asked where his father was and she said out back in the workshop. Go tell him it's time for supper. The boy noticed the empty bottle on the counter, beneath the high cabinet where his father kept his whiskey, and he picked up the bottle and unscrewed the cap and sniffed and it burned through his nose and his mother laughed when he winced and then told him that should teach you all you need to know about that stuff. Don't ever bother with it. Not now not ever. And then the smile left her face and her eyes drifted out of the kitchen window and into the backyard. Her eyes drifted toward the workshop where his father hid most days when he came home from work. Sometimes the buzz of a saw or pounding of a hammer but mostly silence from the workshop. Her eyes drifted and an emptiness came across her face.

She lowered her eyes. Turned on the faucet and washed her hands. Closed her eyes and touched her wet fingertips to her eyelids and held them there, drops of water running down her wrists and from her cheeks and so silent as she paused with her fingers against her eyelids as if commanding time and space to wait for her. Only wait for her for a moment until she was ready again. Colburn knew to leave her alone when she was like this and he backed out of the kitchen and walked across the backyard. He called for his dad before he got there. It's time to eat. Momma said come on. Sometimes he liked going into the workshop. When the radio was playing and his father was sweating in the middle of some time killing project and his father would let him drive a nail or wipe a paintbrush and there was a calm in his father then that he recognized at no other time. Random specks of light against the darkness he carried. And because of this darkness he did not like going into the workshop when there was no sound. Because that was when he would find his father sitting in a folding chair, hunched over with his elbows resting on his knees and a bottle hanging from his hand and blood red eyes and the voice of some other man saying to him, what do you want? Huh? What the hell do you want? And he would back out of the open door and turn and go inside as quickly as he could and say to his mother he's not ready to come in yet and then it would be the next day at the breakfast table before he saw his father again.

On this day there was no sound but he was still running for touchdowns in his mind when he came to the door of the workshop. He reached for the handle but then he paused. Wondered why the door was closed in the heavy heat and he peeked through the slats of the door and saw only shadow. He looked over his shoulder toward the kitchen window and his mother moved back and forth, setting the table and pouring tea into ice filled glasses and he touched his hand to the door handle again and he pulled the door open. He reached inside the door to turn on the light switch but that was when he heard the grunting and the exit of breath. Slices of daylight between the wall planks that cut across his wrestling father as he swung from the ceiling beam of the shed, his ankles bent like a ballerina's and his toes batting against the top of a stool and his face red and spit down the sides of his mouth as the noose squeezed his throat. The boy's eyes went wide and he stepped back and hit his head against the doorframe and his father grunted and choked and smacked at his own throat and face and tried to say something but he could only wave the boy toward him. He waved the boy toward him and Colburn came forward and from a small stack of bricks in the corner of the shed he grabbed two and set them on top of the stool and tried to set his father's feet upon them but his father kicked the bricks away. Slapped at the back of Colburn's head and with another quick wave he motioned him away. Motioned to the other side of the workshop and tried to communicate some impossible message but he was only grunting and spitting and dying. The tips of his toes tapping against the top of the stool and this great moment of indecision and Colburn stared up at his father and into his bulging eyes. He didn't run or scream, as if invisible hands covered his mouth and held him by the shoulders and arms. The ceiling beam creaked with the weight of his father struggling against time and gravity and the dust danced in the slanting light. And then Colburn jerked his head and jerked his shoulders as if to break free from hands that held him and he surged forward and kicked the stool out from under his father.

He backed away. Met his father's eyes one last time. And then he stepped out of the workshop, closing the door behind him. He stood in the yard. Watching his mother move from the stove to the table, oven mitts on her hands and holding a casserole dish. She set the dish in the middle of the table and then she looked out of the window. Caught Colburn staring at her and she gave him a half smile, a half smile he had seen many times that was a poor mask for sadness and when there was silence inside the workshop, he crossed the yard and went inside to get her.

1976

2

THE FOULRUNNING CADILLAC ARRIVED CHUGGING into the town limits of Red Bluff, the car having struggled out of the Delta flatlands and into the Mississippi hill country, the ups and downs of the landscape pushing the roughriding vehicle beyond what was left of its capabilities. The engine finally died as they drove closer to the handful of streets that made up the downtown and the long car rolled to a stop at the edge of the post office parking lot. The smoke curling around the hood and then forming a sloppy cloud that was carried away by an early summer wind. A hiss from the engine. The smell of gasoline. The man and woman sat in the front seat and the boy sat in the back. Eyes out of open windows. Thin faces of submission.

'Where we at?' the woman said.

'Right here,' the man answered.

A woman in a dull blue uniform came out of the post office with a package under her arm. Paused and removed her glasses and looked at the car. No hubcaps. Small dents in the doors. The back fender held in place by a twisted coat hanger. The man leaned his head out of the window and snorted and spit. She shook her head and frowned and then walked across the parking lot and climbed into the boxlike postal vehicle and drove away.

'I'm hungry,' the woman in the car said. 'What we got back there?'

The boy passed up a cupcake wrapped in cellophane. It was lopsided and the icing had melted against the wrapper but she took it and tore it open.

'Gimme a bite,' the man said. But she opened her mouth wide and stuck the entire cupcake inside, the chocolate squishing from the sides of her mouth as she chewed.

The boy got out. Then the man and woman did the same. They gathered at the front of the car, the hissing having died away. The man got down on his knees and looked underneath. A drip in the front and a drip in the back. Then he stood and without a word he started walking and the woman and boy followed. Three gangly figures. The woman's clothes too big and the boy's clothes too small and the man pulling at his chin and stroking a patchy beard. They moved like revenants along the sidewalk. Each with the same spindled limbs and sunken mouth and leathery skin. They passed a church. A feed store. A hardware store. And then empty buildings. For every storefront with an open sign there were three more that provided only shells, the small town mired in the purgatory of what had been and was to come.

A bell jingled when they walked into the drugstore. The pharmacist in a white coat looked up from his perch in the back. A teenage girl with a ponytail sat on a stool behind the counter smacking gum and reading a magazine and when she smelled them she held her breath until they walked past and then she wrinkled her nose and fanned the magazine under it.

'You need some help?' the pharmacist called. His hair was thin and silver and glasses and pens stuck up from his coat pocket. None of them answered the pharmacist as they shuffled from aisle to aisle looking at batteries and cough drops. Wasting as much time as they could in the cool air. The drugstore was silent but for the moving of the pharmacist and the girl, and the woman whispered I wish I could lay down right here and go to sleep.

'Drugstores used to have ice cream and sandwiches,' the man said. 'Y'all got that?'

'We do not,' the pharmacist said.

'How come?'

'Because we don't.'

'They got sandwiches at the café,' the girl said. She set her magazine down and moved from behind the counter and to the door. Holding it open as if they had asked her to ready for their exit.

'You must be passing through,' the pharmacist said.

'Not no more,' the woman answered.

'Might turn out to be home,' the man said. His face dirty and he stared at the pharmacist with his black burrowed eyes as he walked along the middle aisle and closer to him. He mindlessly picked up a box of tissues and held it up and said how much for this.

'Café is right down that way,' the pharmacist said and he waved his hand toward the door. 'You can't eat a box of tissues.'

The man tossed the box on the floor. Grabbed another from the shelf and did the same. The woman was on one side of the store shoving a pack of clean underwear under her shirt and the boy was on the other side shoving candy bars down his pants.

'Leave them boxes right there,' the man proclaimed. 'I'm

gonna come back and get them after we get to this café y'all keep hollering about. I remember right where I left them. Don't let nobody buy them out from under me.'

'Get on out of here,' the pharmacist said. He had slid a step to his right. Closer to the telephone. 'I mean it.'

'So do I.'

The man then turned around and strolled along the middle aisle and toward the open door. The boy and woman met him there and as they left the drugstore the man poked his finger into the belly of the teenage girl who was still holding open the door and he said I think I'll come on back here pretty soon and get another look at you.

The woman was asleep across the back seat with her arm draped across her face. The man sat on the trunk smoking a cigarette, his eyes out into the twilight and his mind on the argument he and the woman had two days before. Their squatting time up in the farmhouse. A gray beard in overalls holding the shotgun on them and walking them to the property line. The woman holding the little boy and the man and the older boy with their hands held above their heads. Walking to the spot in the woods where they had hidden the car and getting in and driving down the dirt road as the shotgun fired a final warning into the air. Getting to a gas station and sitting there with the windows up while a slanting rain blew across the Delta and he gave the boy a dollar and said go inside and get us some canned meat and some Cokes. When the boy was gone the man said to her we can't feed everybody. We got to cut loose. The little boy asleep in her arms. His mouth open and his lips dry. We can't do this shit no more. It was rudimentary math to him. The simple equation of not enough to go around and too much weight to carry in this life and he had never trusted that any of his blood flowed through the child anyway.

That night he stared into the twilight and justified it all as he smoked a cigarette and listened to the crickets. He had known before he even brought up the idea that she would give in. That she'd agree. Had to lighten the load. And she had agreed, more easily than even he thought she would.

They had left the little boy in the afternoon. Naked but for his diaper. Dropping a backpack on the ground next to him stuffed with wadded shirts and diapers. Little green army men. A scrap of paper with his scribbled name. The woman knocking on the back door of the donation store and running around and getting in the car, not looking back at the child. A hand covering her eyes as they drove out of the parking lot. Before dark she was stabbed with regret, crying all night as they sat in the car. Parked down some backroad. The older boy unable to look at them knowing what they had done and climbing over a fence and walking out into a pasture and lying down in the wet grass. The storm having blown away and leaving a long dark sky and a thousand stars. And in the empty night the boy could still hear her crying. Sometimes in whimpers and sometimes in violent thrusts when she pounded her fist against the car and the man saying I don't wanna hear it no more and she had taken the back of his hand across her face and then fought him until he got her pinned against the car window and he spoke calmly to her then. You'd better stop or I'll kill you.

The man finally got her to be quiet by promising everything he had promised to begin with. The little boy will be safer somewhere else and we will get the hell out of here and go into Tennessee. I told you I got people up in Tennessee. We got a place we can stay and we can figure it all out then. She knew he was lying but believing him anyway as a way to suffer her guilt and then waking up in the Cadillac the next day and driving.

He didn't expect to hear about it again and now here they were. Not even making it out of Mississippi. But they had done it. One less to worry about and he wished he could do the same for himself. Drop himself off at somebody's door and let them find him. Take care of him. Feed him. Give him somewhere to sleep. But he was too mean and ugly and all he wanted was to strike back at the world. Get this goddamn car running and leave them here and I should've done that in the first place. Should've taken the little boy all by myself over to the Salvation Army store. Should've never let her go with me even though she begged to be the one to do it. To touch him last. Should've never gone back and got the big one. Should've gone alone and kept goddamn going and left them to figure out their own life.

The woman woke and climbed out of the backseat. Joined him and took a cigarette from the pack lying on the trunk. A kid on a bicycle came along the sidewalk. A dog with its tongue dragging followed behind. The man flicked away his cigarette and asked the kid if anything in this shithole town was open after dark and the kid pedaled on in silence. The boy had spent the day walking around the town and he had found a shopping cart and he rattled into the parking lot, the cart filled with aluminum cans, half a loaf of bread, a handful of paperback books. The man hopped down from the trunk. Took out the bread and nodded toward the books.

'You learn to read?' he asked the boy.

'Leave him alone,' the woman said. The man pulled a piece of bread from the sack and shoved it in his mouth and when the woman reached for the sack, he snatched it away. She then picked up the pack of cigarettes and said you can kiss these goodbye and he changed his mind and passed her the bread. She took a slice for herself and gave one to the boy. It smelled funny but they were standing there in a triangle eating when the cruiser with the star on the side came along the street. The headlights like two bright eyes in the dustblue shift from day to night.

3

THE CRUISER TURNED INTO THE parking lot. Pulled alongside the busted Cadillac. The engine and the headlights turned off and then Myer stepped out. He took off his hat and held the brim with both hands as he walked over to them. Pantlegs tucked inside his boots. A slight limp. Deep lines around the eyes of his sunworn face.

'You got a little hitch in your giddyup,' the man said. 'That's nice of you to notice.'

Myer waited on him to say something else but the man stuck another bite of bread in his mouth and the three of them chewed with no regard to the sheriff or his car or anything in the world at all. Finally Myer said it looks like you're having some trouble. Been sitting here a good while. I can get you towed over to the garage. The man finished the bread and shook his head at the sheriff.

'We fine,' he said.

'We ain't fine,' the woman said.

'Hush.'

'You hush.'

'Where you heading?' Myer asked. He began to move around them, an examining walk around the Cadillac. Looking inside.

'Tennessee,' the woman said.

'Yeah. Tennessee,' the man added.

'What part?'

The man scratched at the back of his neck.

Myer made the lap around the vehicle and stood there close to them. He eyed the woman and then the boy.

'How old are you, son?' he asked.

'Fifteen. Sixteen.'

'You don't know?'

'He knows,' the woman said. She moved to the boy and put her hand on his shoulder. 'He's just messin with you. That's all.'

'We ain't done nothing,' the man said. His words quick as if he had been prodded by something sharp.

'I didn't say you did.'

'Well then.'

'But you are broke down on government property.'

'Tell it to the car.'

'I by God am telling it to you,' Myer said. He set his hat on top of the trunk and put his hands on his hips. 'I came down here to see if we might help you get going but you don't seem interested in my help so I'll try something else. You the one who went in Jimmy Guy's drugstore today and touched his granddaughter?'

'Don't know.'

'Don't know what?'

'This Jimmy Guy fellow.'

The sheriff huffed. Laughed a little.

'Stop it, 'the woman said and she poked at the man's shoulder.

'I ain't stopping nothing. We ain't done nothing.'

The sheriff stepped closer to him. He was a head taller.

Twentysomething years older but a figure of health against the scrawny and hardworn man.

'Okay. I won't ask you anything else. I'll just tell you. You went in that drugstore. You put your hand on that girl and you threatened that girl.'

'That's a lie.'

'You said you'd be coming back for her.'

'That's a goddamn lie.'

'I'm telling you what I was told and I can't find a reason not to believe it.'

'I ain't touched her. I ain't made her no promises. You can ask them two standing right here with us.'

'I ain't asking you anything else. From here on it's telling.' A well of spit filled the man's mouth and he held it. Wanting to let it fly right into the sheriff's face. But he held it. Swallowed. He nodded and said yes sir, knowing that was how to get rid of him.

Myer eased back. Picked up his hat and tapped the trunk with his index finger and said open this up for me.

'It's just our stuff,' the woman said.

'Open it.'

The man took the key from the ignition. Came around to the trunk and opened it. The trunk was a mess of wadded clothes and blankets. Pots and pans. Gallon jugs of water. Empty bottles and cans. A hatchet and lengths of rope and cans of baked beans and corn. Myer poked at the clothes and shifted around a few items and then he closed the trunk. Wiped his hand on his shirt.

'Now,' he said. 'Back to where I started. Do y'all need some help with this car?'

'We don't need no help,' the man said.

'Yes we do,' the woman said. 'But unless you got a mechanic who's gonna fix it out of the goodness of his heart we probably gonna have to let it sit here.'

'You can't let it sit here. I already told you,' the sheriff answered. He then rubbed his chin. Raised his eyes into the evening sky and then looked again at the woman. Looked at the boy who was taking the last slice of bread from the sack. 'Let me see what I can do in the morning. Maybe we can work something out. We'll figure out a way to get you folks back on your way.'

'Yes sir,' the man said.

'You got somewhere to sleep?'

The woman pointed at the Cadillac.

'All right,' the sheriff said. 'I'll be back in the morning.' He nodded to them and set his hat on his head. Walked back to the cruiser and got in. His headlights shining on them as he backed out of the parking lot, their eyes flashing in the light like the eyes of animals hidden and staring from the dark of the wood.

4

As soon as the woman and boy had fallen asleep in the backseat, the man carefully opened the car door and slipped out, leaving the door open so as not to wake them. He walked the sidewalks and the alleys. He walked through yards and looked into cars parked in driveways. He slipped in and out of the shadows, searching for some answer. And then he quit. I'll leave them there, he thought. And he began to walk out of town. No idea of which direction he was going and only coins in his pocket and the town shrunk behind him. He was missing a front row of teeth and was perpetually smacking at his upper lip with his bottom lip, a sucking rhythm that kept the woman sitting right on the edge of anger, the sound a constant reminder to her of this life that they lived but as he walked he listened to the smacking as if it were some notice that he was alive. A lone effigy moving through the moonlight. He walked and wondered and then imagined falling into a big black hole that had no bottom, falling with his arms and legs spread wide and no fear of what was below. He turned and looked back at the few faint lights of town and then he kept walking until he came to the valley.

The moonshine gave a pale light across a land covered in kudzu. The rich green depths and rises and falls of trees and hillsides long since conquered by the timeless vines. The man gazed across the great expanse of green, captivated by the reach of the kudzu. By the multitude of heart shaped leaves that seemed to wave to him as the night wind swept down through the valley. He stood on the road and the kudzu came right up to its edge. One step from the bumpy asphalt. He knelt and took the end of a vine in his fingers and it was thick like a pencil and rough and scratchy. He then touched a leaf. Slick and smooth. He snapped it from the vine and held it flat in his palm and stroked it with his rough fingertips as if trying to soothe it to sleep.

He carried the leaf as he kept walking, the road turning in a long curve that wrapped around the valley. The vines hanging down from clumps of forest that served like some curtain into the backstage world below the kudzu and into it the man entered. Standing there among the trees. Moving deeper inside. The kudzu canopy above blocking out the moonglow and in the dark he heard things and imagined more things and he hurried back out to the road. His breaths quicker. His heart quicker. The sides of his mouth bent up in a smile. He no longer wanted to leave. He no longer wanted to walk off into the night. He picked more leaves from the vines and he squeezed them in his hands as he hurried back toward town, the eastern sky beginning to change from black to blue. He kept looking over his shoulder as he walked as if to make sure the valley had not been part of a dream and just before first light he returned to the car. He reached into the open window of the backseat and shook the woman by her shoulder and did the same to the boy. They were slumped against each other and he pushed at her until her eyes opened and he said get up. Both of you. Get up and start pushing. I found us somewhere.

5

MYER STOOD WITH HIS HANDS on his hips in the empty space in the parking lot where the car had been. He tried to believe he had imagined it. The man and woman and boy and their old Caddy. His offer for help, their rejection of it. Maybe the damn thing did run. Maybe they cranked it and drove off. Wouldn't be the first time that crew lied to somebody. Maybe they're headed toward Tennessee like the man said. Myer kicked at a rock and then looked down at his own shadow from the morning sun. His shoulders slumped to ease the pain that lived in his back, his tall frame having settled over the years in ways that pinched. You need to get out of the cruiser and walk around every now and then, his wife told him. You need to do your stretches like the doctor said. You need to stand up straight and be the tall and proud man God made you.

You need to hush, he'd tell her. I've grown old and no amount of walking or stretching is gonna fix that. Old and lazy ain't the same thing, she'd tell him. No matter how bad you want it to be.

He stared at his shadow and he straightened up. Pulled his shoulders back. Raised his arms over his head and stretched. He then bent at the waist and let his arms dangle toward the ground. It felt good and when he raised himself he kept his shoulders up high. Walked a lap around the cruiser and he saw the wet circles on the ground from the drips and leaks from their car and he knew they were gone from this parking lot but they were not gone.

He got in the cruiser and drove around downtown. Looking in alleys and behind storefronts and then making his way into the neighborhoods. On one side of the railroad tracks were the woodframe houses with their paint chipping and porches sagging. Tricycles in front yards and potted ferns on porch steps and magnolia trees growing wild as if reaching out to hold the houses erect. On the other side of the tracks the streets were lined with short houses. Stubborn, meanlooking structures of brick and mortar. He waved to old women in housecoats who sat on porch swings drinking coffee. He waved to mothers and their children playing in front yards. He waved to men climbing in their trucks, lunch pails in hand. But he saw no ragged Cadillac and none of the ragged people that arrived with it and as he lapped back around and parked in front of the downtown café, he wasn't even sure what he'd do if he found them.

6

TWO MILES SEPARATED THE VALLEY from town and each day the woman and the boy pushed the shopping cart along the bumpy pavement between. Sometimes the woman would start crying and then she would stop. Bite at her own arm as if to redirect the pain. The boy would wait for her. No words between them. Only walking again when she was done. Once they reached town, they moved the shopping cart onto the smoother sidewalks and then set it inside an alley, where they cupped their hands and drank from a water spigot. Washed their arms and faces and necks. Sat down with their backs against the brick wall in the shade of the alley and hoped for good luck in the garbage bins behind the café and the market. Hoped for a thirsty crowd the night before at the cinderblock bar and all the empty bottles and cans they could exchange for cents on the dollar. Knocked on the back door of the café for day-old bread or softening vegetables. But most of all they hoped to be able to mill around and do what they had to do without sharp voices commanding them to go away.

The man ate whenever they returned with food. He mumbled to and pawed at the woman. He ignored the boy. He wandered into town at night. He slept. He and the woman and the boy had been so long detached and displaced that he had come to think of the three of them as some other species. Creatures of their own making. It was not much more than the existence of a dog but it had begun to evolve into something else in the starry nights when he walked along the road back toward the hovel. After having milled about town, talking to the reflection of his winnowed form in store windows and watching the people in the bar through the glass door and waiting for the redhaired woman to come out with the bottles and cans. After having smoked nubs of discarded cigarettes and after having pissed on the same shrubs in front of the Baptist church night after night he would then make his way back out of the town. The days growing long and the heat stretching into the night and he sometimes sang bits and pieces of songs he could remember and sometimes cussed a passing car but in recent days he had begun to keep his mouth shut and listen as he moved in the dark. The thrum of the cicadas and the howls and screeches that pealed across the land.

He did not know when he had begun to hear the voice only that it had started. It was not there and then it was. And he stopped and stared at the stars and the bright round moon and he listened to it. In those empty nights he walked with his mouth shut and when the wind blew he opened his palms to feel the push of the air and he sometimes stopped and knelt as if his spirit had been moved and there was no longer the world before him but there was only the world beyond flesh and bone and he would return to the hovel on the nights when the voice was the most licentious and he would slide his hands around the woman's throat as she grunted and rocked in her sleep, his dirty hands around her dirty neck and he felt the pulse of her throat and felt her life surging through his and the crux of this lowdown existence they had created for themselves and he would squeeze his hands until she slapped them away as if they were fatal creatures of her dreams crawling on her neck. He would then sit back. Look at his own hands, black and blurry in the dark. He would put them around his own throat and whisper is this what you mean? Is this what you mean? And he would wait for the voice to answer as he squeezed his own throat until his air was short and he would release and fall out of the open door of the car. His face against the ground and a single trail of vine stretching down into their crude camp, a vine that he would reach for and hold between his grimy fingernails as if it were a lifeline of salvation.

Then he would crawl over to the boy who slept on a pile of blankets. This thing that lived and breathed and shared his same bent brow and sunken eyes. This thing that felt like both a part of him and an intrusion and he imagined he was looking at himself and if he could go back and rid himself of this life he would accept the opportunity with his hands ready to kill. The man would strike a match, the quick flick then the tiny light on the boy, his mouth open and his sunsoaked skin and the voice would whisper. Reach in there and grab him and pull him out and the man would take his index finger and slide it inside the boy's mouth that was open in slumber, feel his hot breath and the rhythm of his breathing and he would drop the match so that he could pin down the boy's head with his other hand while he reached down into his soul to snatch it away but each time he dropped the match he lost his nerve and he scooted away from the boy.

There was no longer sleep and he explored through the night, moving back to the road and walking around the edge of the valley, staring at the house lights on the hillsides and each night moving a little closer. The houses like islands spread far apart and separated by the waves of kudzu. He squatted in the road and watched the sleeping houses, imagining the warm bodies between the sheets and the fucking or fighting that went on in the waking hours. He moved into their yards and leaned against their trees. Looked into their windows. Smelled their sheets on the clothesline. Sat on the rockers on their porches. Moved flowerpots from one side of the yard to the other. Opened their car doors and hid their bicycles behind trees. Doing just enough to make them realize someone had been there.

7

THE FLATBED TRUCK TURNED ONTO Main Street and bumped across the bricked street, the bricks shifting and odd like rows of teeth. The flatbed was covered in a shapeless heap of scrap metal and aluminum poles and rebar and toolboxes, lines of rope pulled tight across the heap like some rugged web and heads turned with the clatters and clangs and Colburn nodded in reply to their curiosity. At the end of Main Street there stood an antebellum home and a sign in the yard read TOWN HALL. Colburn parked the truck. Killed the engine and smoked another cigarette. He asked himself again if this was really what he wanted to do.

Colburn called himself an industrial sculptor when he tried to explain it to the woman at town hall. He showed her the newspaper article from the *Jackson Daily News* about Red Bluff giving away abandoned downtown storefronts to artists and musicians and writers, to be used as studios or workspaces. The only stipulations being you had to keep residence in town and keep the buildings maintained. When she didn't take it from his hand he shook it at her, as if to prove why he was here but she only shrugged and said it's all true. If you say you're an artist then I guess you're an artist. She walked him down to the building without any more questions, her lips pressed tightly together as if knowing she was on the wrong end of a bad deal. She unlocked the door and waved her hand around at the empty space and then she had him sign a piece of paper and she gave him the keys.

'Is that it?' he asked.

'I suppose,' she said. 'We got no precedent. You're the only one that's bothered to show up.'

He spent his first days driving the flatbed truck around the countryside, searching for forgotten machinery or vinecovered cars sunk back into the land. He pulled into driveways as heads looked around curtains and then he knocked on doors and asked for hubcaps leaned against trees or rusted cars sitting on blocks with wild flowers growing up through their open hoods. Sunworn men looked at him with thoughtless stares as barefoot children peeked out from behind trees or studied what he had already accumulated on the flatbed. The men would shake their heads and say I need this or I need that when he pointed toward truck doors attached to no truck or radiators wrapped in white blossoms or boats with rusted bottoms that were long since incapable of flotation. Colburn's cause was helped when wives wearing aprons around their waists stood in doorways with their hands on their hips and sometimes stomped a foot. Sometimes cleared a throat. It was then that men would nod and say fine. You can take it but one day I'll wish you hadn't. The random pieces and parts more than metal and iron. More than surfaces of rust and grime. To the men they were memories of better days gone by or suggestions of the possibilities of futures they were now certain would never come. He hauled away their pasts and their hopes, strapped into the back of the truck.

Colburn worked in the broad front room and slept on a cot

in a smaller room with a door that opened into an alley. He had a sink and a toilet and his clothes were piled in laundry baskets. He ate lunch at the café a block away but it was not open in the evening and the garbage bin in the alley was filled with plastic food wrappers and bottles from whatever he felt like eating from the gas station.

The front of his building was a large window and he liked working with the honest light of day and he liked them stopping with shopping bags in their arms or cigarettes in the side of their mouths or holding their children and watching him through the window. The sparks in a storm of red and orange as he cut through castiron pipes or smoothed the jagged edges of sheet metal. The blue smoke surrounding him like a cape and he would stop to look at them from behind his giant, rectangle welding mask, this creator of fire and smoke who was sweatsoaked and alien and he would wave a gloved hand but they would not wave back and instead took his kindly gesture as a sign to turn and leave.

But Celia did not leave when he noticed her there. Standing alone on a late afternoon and a southern breeze pushing her red curls across her face. One hand propped on her hip and the other hand touching the window with her fingertips. A tall and twisted roll of rebar serving as the centerpiece for his new creation and cut strips of barbed wire hanging from steel pipes that sprang from the top of the rebar like reaches of steel growth. The reek of smoke and Colburn with his shirt off and bathed in sweat and he set the blowtorch aside. Took off the welder's mask. Picked up his shirt and wiped his face and scrubbed at his long hair that was matted against his head. He stepped back from the sculpture and took a pack of cigarettes from the top of a stool. He smoked and looked upon the evolution of his creation and thought it might be some type of tree in a treeless world or perhaps a thing that children imagined to be hiding in closets.

He sat down on the stool and looked over to the window. Her hair across her eyes and jeans with rips at the knees and bare feet. He waved and she moved her hand from the window. Kept the other hand on her hip and took several steps along the sidewalk as she raised her index finger and beckoned him to follow her.

And he did. He hurried to put his shirt on and he hurried out of the building and she walked half a block ahead, pausing at each corner to make sure he saw the direction she was going. He followed her through the downtown streets and noticed one of her back pockets was torn away and the bottoms of her feet were brown and she stopped when she came to the bar. A long and squat cinderblock building that may have been mistaken for an ill-fated attempt at a bomb shelter except for the halfmoon and scattering of stars that was painted along the side. She went in the front door, looking over her shoulder one last time to see if he was still there. When Colburn walked inside it took a few seconds for his eyes to adjust from light to shadow and once they came clear, he found her nestled behind the bartop, sitting on top of the beer cooler with her knees pulled up and sticking through the rips in her jeans. A bottle of beer for her and one for him already on the bar. A silver Zippo stacked on top of a pack of cigarettes placed between the bottles. Come on over here, she said.

8

HE CROSSED THE BARROOM FLOOR and sat on a stool. He picked up the beer and drank. Something twangy played on the jukebox and two old men sat at the other end of the bar with lowhung heads and eyed Colburn.

'Do you know what you are?' the bartender asked. Her hair long and red and curling in tendrils.

He shook his head.

'The strange animal in the zoo.'

Colburn drank again. Looked around. The smoky light. The liquor bottles on the shelves behind the bar. A smokestained ceiling. A clock on the wall that was an hour behind.

'Cat got your tongue?' one of the old men said.

'I wasn't asked a question.'

'Well you are now.'

'What question is that?' Colburn said.

'What you doing over there with all the smoke and sparks?'

He rubbed at his neck. Lifted his damp shirt and wiped his damp face. Then he stood and pulled a couple of wrinkled dollars from his pocket and laid them on the bar.

'What's that for?' Celia asked.

'The beer.'

'It's on me.'

'This your place?'

'Every old inch.'

Celia uncrossed her legs and hopped off the cooler. She picked up the wrinkled bills and flattened them on the bar and ran her hand across to smooth them.

'I've seen you riding around out by the valley. You go by my house.'

'Which one is that?'

'Wouldn't you like to know?'

He waited for her to laugh but she didn't. Neither did the old men. She picked up the Zippo and flipped it open and shut and seemed to be waiting for him to say something but he didn't know what that was.

'So,' she said. 'What do you do with that stuff when you're done?'

'I try to sell it. Mostly in New Orleans or Memphis when I get enough put together.'

'People buy that shit?'

'Every now and then.'

'And what if they don't?'

'I go off on a welding job somewhere for a few months.'

'I'm kidding when I call it shit.'

He shrugged. Drank again.

'Why here?' she said.

'What do you mean?'

'This town? You can fire up a blowtorch anywhere.'

'It's free,' one of the old men said.

'That's not it,' Celia said. 'It's been free for months and we've drawn a crowd of one.'

'I used to live here,' Colburn said. He then reached for a cigarette and stuck it in his mouth as if to keep himself from saying any more.

'Really?'

He held out his hand. She passed him the Zippo and he flicked it open and lit the cigarette.

'What's your name?'

'You don't know me.'

'I bet one of us sitting here knows you or your momma and daddy.'

'No,' Colburn said. 'You don't. It was a long time ago.'

'Everything was a long time ago,' one of the old men said. 'It just feels like it,' the other said.

Colburn raised the beer one last time and drained it. He then set the empty bottle on the bar.

'I've been here all my life,' Celia said. 'We look about the same age, give or take. Try me.'

'Tell me yours first.'

'Celia.'

'Colburn,' he said.

Celia paused. Cut her eyes down the bar to the old men. 'Colburn what?' she said.

'Colburn Evans.'

She picked up the bills and folded them. Pushed them across the bar. He picked them up and stuck them down in his pocket and waited to see if she would answer. But she only looked at him from behind the curls dangling across her eyes. He set the Zippo down and said thanks and then he walked out of the bar, a wave of daylight sweeping across the concrete floor as the door opened and closed.

'That boy is in for a surprise,' one of the old men said. 'Thinking won't nobody know who he belongs to.'

'Yep,' the other answered.

Celia picked up the Zippo. Rubbed it between her fingers.

Touching where he had touched. Then she set it back down
on the bar and her eyes moved to the door.

9

CELIA RAN THE OLD MEN out and locked the door of the bar and left a note stuck to it that said I'll be right back. She climbed into her car and drove away from town and along a thin and badly patched strip of asphalt that wound through the hillsides. In the easy light of the afternoon she held her hand out of the window and moved it up and down with the pulse of the wind. She came around a bend and to the beginnings of where the kudzu had taken over and she slowed as she drove along the edge of the valley and then she came to a small clearing where her house sat back from the road. A dozen pecan trees in neat rows in front of the house. Around the edge of the property the kudzu had been cut back and gave the house and the trees and the land the appearance of resting inside a heavy green cushion.

She turned onto the gravel driveway that split the pecan trees. She parked and got out and stepped onto the porch. There were a couple of wicker chairs. Empty wine bottles with candles stuck in the necks. An overfilled ashtray and a loose stack of magazines across a small table between the chairs.

The outline of the neon hand filled the front window. Inside the hand were the words PSYCHIC READINGS. When the hand was turned on it glowed in blue and the letters glowed in yellow and promised comfort to the wandering souls willing to pay. But it had not glowed since her mother turned it off twenty years before.

Celia crossed the porch and went inside. The wide hallway and tall ceilings. Slanting hardwood floors. Big windows and thick crown molding. Slowturning ceiling fans. She passed through the house as if she were a stranger. Her fingers touching the wideframe of the doorways as she moved from room to room. Her eyes into the corners. Behind doors. Looking for the ghosts she had always believed to be there, unwilling to play hide-and-seek as a child as she supposed the small and dark places were occupied. Unwilling to sleep with the closet door open. Unwilling to trust her mother when she told her the sounds in the night are only the wind sweeping across the valley or the howls of lonely animals. She had lived in this same house her entire life and she knew the fifty-seven creaks in the floor and the rattle of each window. She knew which shadows would fall at what time of day and she knew how to talk herself out of a nightmare but there were voices of the past talking to her now and she halfexpected their wraithlike figures to be there waiting for her.

She walked through the kitchen and out of the back door. She moved down the steps and across the yard that fell in a slope toward the kudzu and she imagined her mother there. Standing at the edge. Her feet into the vines. Staring out at the valley. And Celia remembered the times she had come home and found her mother further out, waist deep in the tangle of vines. Helping her climb out and getting her back inside the house and telling her again and again. Mother, you can't go out there. I don't want you outside by yourself. But her mother no longer understanding and answering her with head nods and a placid expression. And then saying I need to go talk to him. I need to talk to that man.

What man? Celia would ask. But she knew what man. The man who had knocked on their door in the middle of the night, however many years before, in the days when Celia's mother kept the hand glowing and kept the door open to those looking for answers. In the days when her mother was healthy and happy. The man had knocked on the door and then she had taken him into the front room of the house where she did the readings. A round wooden table in the center of the room and a long table against the wall that was covered with candles that glowed like a choir of flamelight. A stick of burning incense and a solitary lamp in the corner of the room with a red lightbulb. And he had been the last one she had ever given a reading to and it had been the last night the blue hand shined in the dark because days later after he hung himself, her mother did not want to do it anymore.

Celia shook free from the image of her mother and went back inside and into her mother's reading room. The tables still there. The solitary lamp still there. In the corner of the rooms at a wooden trunk and Celia knelt next to it and opened it. Inside were the notebooks where her mother had kept records of the visitors and the dates they visited and what they had talked about and what she thought they needed to hear, notebooks that her mother had torn the pages from in the final months of her life as she berated herself. Tearing the pages out and then going back and tearing them again as if one fury was not enough. And then writing new notes and throwing them into the pile and when Celia would get her into the bed for the night she would go and look in the trunk for what her mother had written and she found fragments of sentences and sometimes only words.

Before he goes.

Last sunset.

Liar.

Man in the dark.

Scraps of paper with words only her mother could understand and then when her mother was too weak to get out of bed Celia would sit with her and hold a notebook while her mother scribbled and scratched a pencil across the paper. Let it out, Celia would tell her. Let it all out. Wanting her to die with her mind at peace.

Celia closed the trunk. She sniffed. Then she crawled to the wall and sat with her back against it. She held her hands in her lap. Outside the birds sat in the pecan trees and sang afternoon love songs but they were interrupted by the sound of the diesel engine of the flatbed as it chugged around the valley. The thrum of the engine came closer and Celia scooted across the floor and looked out of the front window, through the fingers of the hand. She then saw Colburn pass in front of the house and her eyes followed until he was around the bend and out of sight and all was quiet again.

She stood. Stepped back and looked at the hand. Then she plugged it in. A silver chain hung from the side and she held it between her fingers and pulled. There was a click. An electric buzz. Finally there was a flicker and then little pops and crackles and the hand began to glow, the blue outline of the fingers and palm. Her cheeks rose in an unconscious smile as the letters came to life. Some of them. After the light had done all it was going to do, she walked outside and stood on the porch. It had drawn his father. She wondered if it would draw him too.

10

IN THE NIGHT COLBURN WALKED the neighborhoods surrounding downtown. Trying to figure out which house it was but they all looked the same. Wanting to see it and not wanting to see it. Every house and every workshop in every town his mother had moved them to in the aftermath of Red Bluff, a rambling existence from one little place to the next during his teenage years as she searched for a place to forget, it had all melted into one generic setting for suicide. But the house was here. Somewhere. And he walked through the night looking and listening. As if his mother's screams would resurrect and pierce the dark and lead him to his haunted home.

11

MYER HAD TAKEN CALL AFTER call. Get these people out of my garbage cans. Get these people off my street. Get these people away from my storefront.

He pulled alongside the woman and the boy as they walked back out of town and toward the valley. Slowing the cruiser and talking to them through the open window. Asking if they needed a ride. But the woman said no and the boy said nothing. He drove ahead, looking for the spot and he found it. The Cadillac camouflaged off the road, inside the trees and draped by the vines. He parked and got out. The woman and boy a quarter of a mile back. He walked down into their camp and the man was lying on his back on the hood. Sound asleep.

'Hey,' Myer said.

The man didn't move. Myer slapped the hood and his head popped up.

'Sit up and let's talk a minute,' he said.

The man wiped at his mouth. Raised himself and slid from the hood. Stretched his arms over his head.

'I thought y'all were gonna get this thing fixed and head on for Tennessee,' Myer said.

'I thought we told you we didn't have no money to fix it.'

'I came back the next morning. Had it worked out with Henry Junior at the garage to have a look at it. Maybe give you some help or a little work to pay it back.'

The man smacked at his gums.

'Where did you say you came from?'

'We didn't say it.'

'Then where'd you come from?'

The man smacked at his forearm as if being bitten. Then he reached into his pocket and pulled out a half-smoked cigarette. He held it in his mouth and crossed his arms.

'Did you hear me?'

'If you would jot down on a slip of paper what you'd prefer me to say, that'd sure speed this along.'

The sound of a rattling cart came closer. Myer walked around the hovel, looking at the scattering of clothes and water jugs and trash.

'Where you come from and I ain't asking again.'

'Somewhere around Tunica.'

'What somewhere?'

'I don't know. All them little shit places out there you can't never figure out their names.'

'You can't live here,' Myer said.

'What the hell do you care?'

The rattling stopped on the roadside. The boy and the woman then came down into the hovel. The woman held a brown bag with a grease spot on the bottom and the boy had taken his shirt off as they finished their walk and it was draped over his shoulder. His ribs and collarbones pushing against his skin.

'He do something?' the woman asked.

'He's a smartass,' Myer said.

'I been knowing that. Did we do something?'

'No.'

'We don't steal nothing.'

'I haven't heard if you did.'

'We ask for work.'

'I just wanted to see where y'all were,' Myer said. 'You come get me when you get ready to get this car fixed. I told him I'd help with it.' He gave the man one more look and then he walked out of the hovel and opened the door of the cruiser. He looked down the road toward town. It seemed a world away.

One of the twins pushed the bicycle and the other swung a hatchet as they walked along the side of the valley road. Myer slowed the cruiser as he approached them, easing close behind and then hitting the siren and with the sudden wail they jumped. The bicycle and the hatchet hit the ground as quick screams came from their identical mouths.

'Damn shit,' one of them yelled.

Myer laughed with his head thrown back, laughing so hard it hurt his back and then the laugh turned to grimace. He shifted in the seat and got himself comfortable again and then he rolled down the window and pulled next to the boys. They picked up the bicycle and hatchet and glared at Myer like little mad men. The same blond hair and the same crooked, homemade haircuts. They both wore jerseys. One number 12 and the other number 32.

'That ain't funny,' one of them said.

'Your momma know you got that hatchet?' Myer said.

'She knows.'

'How's she feeling?'

'Fine I guess.'

'She's got another headache,' the other said.

'Which is it?' Myer said. 'She's fine or down with a headache?'

They looked at each other and shrugged.

'Where you two going?'

'Going to build a fort down in there somewhere,' one said. 'When we doing scouts again?' the other asked.

'I don't know,' Myer said. 'Didn't have but you two and one other show up last time. But maybe we can figure out something to do. Throw up a tent out by my pond and we can fish and build a fire. How'd that be?'

'That'd be fine.'

'Ask your momma.'

They nodded.

'Don't go back that way,' Myer said.

'How come?'

'Somebody else already built a fort. You go on this way.' A length of rope was curled on the floorboard of the cruiser and Myer grabbed it and held it out the window to the twins.

'What's that for?'

'You might need it. More than I do. Just go on this way like I said.'

'Okay.'

Myer shifted into drive and pulled away, watching them in the rearview mirror as they crossed the road and stood at the edge of the valley. Their figures shrinking in the distance. And he wondered if he should have told the twins more about the man and the woman and the boy.

12

THE CAVE AND TUNNEL HAD been dug by slaves in preparation for an approaching war. A place for themselves and their children to hide as they listened to the cannons and the guns and the screams of men. The valley not yet captured by the kudzu but alive with wildflowers and gatherings of maples and pines. A wagon trail weaved up and down the hillsides between cabins with chimneys and in the evening the sun set along the crevice of the valley in a blood-red wash of day to night. Coyotes stood upon the ridges in the moonlight and watched for prey and in the early morning the songs of working women settled into the damp haze like the ballads of lost and foggy souls. The tunnel ran deep beneath the hillside like a thick black vein and it had been dug by torchlight, callused hands driving spades and shovels and pushing wheelbarrows, working all hours of the night after having worked all hours of the day.

In time the opening to the cave had been covered like everything else. The kudzu methodical. Skulking across the land with a demented patience and it had taken a century but the rolling hills were now covered. Along a hillside an old house and chimney held erect beneath its green cover. Down from the bluffs the vines hung like ropes. Small thickets of forest had been conquered decades before, the vines climbing to the highest points and reaching out to the farthest limbs, intertwined and forming slumping canopies. Crippled trees and gathered brush provided mounds and humps across the valley and down below this stretching canvas of green was the blackwood where creatures crawled and sunlight fought through pecks of space between the leaves. A skinny spring ran crooked down a hillside, a rivulet of cold fresh water that arose from between rock and clay and twisted like a silver snake through the dark. And when the wind swept through the valley the leaves moved like ripples across an emerald lake and some claimed to hear a song or a calling or a cry as the wind rose and fell.

The opening was shrouded in a thick blanket of vines and low-hanging limbs and it was more of a hole in the ground. And the man fell into it. His foot found the emptiness and then his body followed, the vines and limbs that covered the entrance held him for a moment before his weight collapsed down into the darkness. He landed softly, fallen leaves forming a cushion, and when he got to his feet he was surprised to find he could raise his hand and touch the edge of the opening.

He tore away the vines and limbs and allowed what little light he could down into the cave. There was space around him wide enough to spread his arms and spin around and touch nothing. The walls were of a dark rich soil and decorated with cuts of rock and jagged tree roots and he poked his fingers into the earth. Rubbed the soil between his fingers. And then he turned in the muted light and saw the black hole of a tunnel.

He moved closer and he took a cautious step inside. The air suddenly cool and a faint wind. He held his hands out in front and moved further into the tunnel. His steps careful and his head brushing against the top of the tunnel and dirt falling down into his hair and ears. He lowered his head and crept further and further in and the light faded and from somewhere deep and dark came a low and steady moan. He paused and looked back over his shoulder, reached out his hand as if to grab a patch of light and carry it with him and he imagined his hands being snatched and his body being dragged along the ground. He turned back toward the dark and listened to the moan. Stared into the black and moved forward with careful steps, hunched down as if readying to be surprised. He stumbled and went down to a knee but was up again quickly and something brushed his shoulder as he stood. He flailed his arms and his knuckles scraped the dirt and rock of the tunnel walls and he let out a quick yelp that echoed and then disappeared as if falling into a well.

He rose and stood still, caught between curiosity and fear. The cool air chilled his skin and he rubbed at his arms and then he called out. Not in words but instead returning the same moan that summoned him. His mouth open and his voice wobbly as he moaned out into the dark and listened for what might come and as he waited he felt the sensation of someone or something standing right in front of him. The cool wind now came in stutters, like a breath in his face. And he imagined the breath pushing through frothy jowls and elongated fangs and he imagined red eyes and sharp ears and outstretched arms waiting to wrap him and drag him deep down into this black world and he took a step back and he felt the figure move with him.

And then he noticed that the moan had stopped and there was only grave silence. He was sweating now and he reached for the tunnel wall so that he could retreat. One careful step at a time. His fingers touching the wall and tripping once but catching himself and moving on until he returned to the dull light and it offered what he had been waiting for. The chance to turn and run.

13

THE BOY BEGAN TO WAKE earlier and go it alone. Leaving the cart behind. Rising from his earth bed and craning his neck and then getting to his feet. Stretching his arms above his head and looking around for something to drink and then brushing the dust and dead leaves from his legs and chest. The man always on his stomach with his face buried in the fold of his arm as if ducking from shellfire and the woman in the backseat with her knees pulled up and her mouth open and stuck in a soundless scream.

When he reached town he sat on a bench in front of the hardware store and he watched. The men pulled up in their work trucks and got out with Styrofoam cups of coffee and cigarettes. Some sat inside the truck cabs and waited, their heads back against the headrests and their eyes closed in final grasps of repose before they had to lay shingles or raise walls or dig ditches for drainage pipes. Soon the sun began to rise and the haze burned away and then came the day's first shadows. Along Main Street cars arrived and slipped into parking spots and store owners opened their storefronts and then returned to sweep the sidewalk and nod to one another. The boy walked the sidewalk and asked them if they needed help. If he could do the sweeping or take out the garbage or do anything that might give a dollar or two but they said

I got it or don't need nothing today, sometimes looking at him when they answered and sometimes not and then they returned inside and left him standing alone on the sidewalk with his hands shoved down into his empty pockets.

His luck came when he began to ask the men in the work trucks if they needed an extra hand. What can you do, they asked. Whatever, he answered. How old are you? When he shrugged the bossman guessed old enough. And then the bossman and the crew would look him up and down. This wild thing that seemed as sunkeyed as a damaged old man yet still possessing the gift of youth. And he climbed into truck beds and took a ride, the warm air whipping around him and his eyes open and tearing and the water stretching from the corners of his eyes like something clean and cool and he did not wipe the tears but let them run until they disappeared into his hairline and he always wanted the job site to be so far away.

But the truck would eventually slow down and then turn into a gravel driveway where there was the skeleton of a house and uneven mounds of dirt. He got out of the truck with the others and they would fasten their toolbelts and he tried to do what they asked him to do. But he had trouble figuring out how to make the hammer or the shovel work the right way and he was ashamed to ask when he was confused or struggling and it was always easy for the bossman to shake his head or make some smartass comment that made the others laugh and when the day was over and they drove back into town it was just as easy to tell the boy I won't need you tomorrow or the next day and the boy would nod as if he understood what he had done wrong and then he would walk away only after their eyes gave him no other choice.

On the days when he worked he returned to the hovel in the late afternoon and he had to listen to the woman berate him for not being there to help her push the cart and he had to listen to the man ask him how much they paid him. When he said I didn't do it right he then had to listen to the man tell him all the reasons he was not worth a goddamn and then the boy would leave them as they finally turned on each other in fits of hunger and frustration. Going down into the valley. Thinking about the ride in the back of the truck and touching the side of his face where the tears had streaked from his eyes.

14

I'M GOING BACK,' THE WOMAN told him. She was leaning against the hood of the Cadillac. Her arms folded in resolution. She and the man were alone.

'Going back where?' the man asked.

'Going back to get him.'

He was sitting on an overturned paint bucket and he stood up.

'You won't.'

'I will.'

'It won't do no good.'

'I don't care.'

'How you figure you're gonna get back?'

'I'm gonna get the sheriff to fix this car. He said he would.'

'He's full of it.'

'Then I'm gonna tell him what we done and he'll take me back.'

'Shit. He'll make one phone call to figure out if you're lying or not and then he'll throw you under the jail.'

'I don't care no more. I been thinking about it. I'm going back to get him and that's the only way I know to do it.'

'It ain't just you. You know that. If it goes bad it'll be the both of us.'

'I said I don't care.'

He walked over and stood next to her. The midday sun fought through the spaces between the vines and trees, leopard spots of light dotting the ground around them. All around the car were piles of trash they kept to start fires. Milk crates filled with the junk the boy found in town and brought back to the hovel. Empty beer cans and cigarette butts and dirty blankets. The woman unfolded her arms and waved her hand at their place here below and she said we're fucking worse than animals and I'm sick of it.

'You think about that for a second,' he said.

'What?'

'The words you said. We're fucking worse than animals. Think they just gonna hand that little boy back to somebody like you. You done run off on him once and you ain't got nowhere to go with him. What you think is gonna happen?'

She folded her arms again. Bit at the side of her mouth.

'Don't you get the sheriff,' he said.

She sniffed.

'I said don't you get the sheriff.'

'I ain't deaf.'

'You done the right thing. We done the right thing. Should've done it with the other one a long time ago.'

'Shut your mouth,' she said. 'Shut your goddamn mouth.'

He backed away from her. Walked around the Cadillac. Tugged at the coat hanger that kept the bumper above ground. He then stared at the back of her head and knew he would come back to the hovel and find her gone. Maybe not today or tomorrow but one day.

'I don't mean it,' he said. 'But you need to settle down.' She didn't answer. She rubbed her hands up and down her arms and thought of the dreams that woke her in the night, dreams of a great pit that lived and breathed and sucked at her feet, taking hold of first her ankles and then her knees and drawing her closer into its depths as she dug her fingers into the ground and clawed to remain above. She wondered if the little boy they had abandoned would one day share these same dreams.

'I can't figure out what to do,' she said. 'It won't leave me.'

'It will. If you let it.'

'That's what I mean to tell you. I don't want to let it. I want to go get him.'

She moved from the car. Slid her feet across the dusty ground and nudged an empty can with her foot.

'You need to think on something else,' he said. 'Let's go somewhere.'

'I ain't walking to town. I'm tired of that too.'

'I got something better.'

'What is it?'

'Something better, that's all. I'll show you.'

15

'I AIN'T GOING IN THERE,' the woman said. She and the man stood together, looking down into the cave opening.

'It's a tunnel.'

'I know. You done told me about it.'

'I figure it might be treasure somewhere in it.'

'I don't care. I ain't going in there.'

'Don't be chicken.'

'I ain't chicken. I just ain't stupid.'

'What's stupid?'

'You mean to ask me what's stupid about going down in a hole you don't know nothing about and walking around in the dark you don't know nothing about?'

'I know about it. I been in there about fifty times.'

'You can do fifty-one like you done them others.'

'How's that?'

'By yourself.'

'Come on.'

'I ain't.'

He kept asking and she kept refusing and her feet remained still. Hands propped on her hips. Her head leaned over and her eyes down into the opening.

'That's why I brought this light,' he said. He held up the kerosene lamp. The boy had brought it back from town in the shopping cart. The glass was cracked and the wick burned down to a black stump. Half an inch of oil swishing around in the basin.

'Come on,' he said again.

She looked up at him. He was licking at the empty space where his front teeth used to be and he stood half-squatted as if getting ready to jump.

'Don't mess with me,' she said.

'I ain't.'

'You got to help me down.'

'I'm fixing to.'

'If there was a treasure you would've done found it.'

'Maybe.'

'You best not mess with me.'

'I said I ain't.'

'You say a lot of shit.'

'You might like it. I bet you ain't been in nothing like this before.'

'You act like you ain't been beside me damn near every day of my life.'

'Not every minute of every day.'

She looked over down into the opening again.

'You go down first and you light that thing,' she said. 'I ain't going in there all dark and shit.'

'Here,' he said and he handed her the lantern. 'Hold it while I get down.'

He grabbed hold of the vines and eased down into the opening. He then reached up and she passed him the lantern.

'Do like I done,' he said.

She took hold of the vines. Crouched and then sat on the edge of the opening with her legs hanging. He wrapped his arms around her legs and she let her weight slide from the edge and he eased her down inside.

'How we supposed to get out?' she asked.

'Same way,' he said.

He pulled a matchbox from his pocket. Removed the cracked glass and struck a match and held it to the wick. The wick smoldered and then turned blue and burned into yellow. He replaced the glass and said we might better hurry. It ain't gonna burn long.

'I ain't going far anyhow.'

'You might change your mind.'

'I ain't.'

'Well. Come on.'

They began down the tunnel. The lantern gave a golden glow and their shadows loomed large against the tunnel walls. The man in front and the woman behind, her fingers hooked around the belt loop of his pants.

'See,' he said. 'Ain't nothing but dark.'

'It don't feel like it. Feels like something else in here.'

'Like what?'

'Like I don't know what. Something mean.'

'You mean animal.'

'No. Worse.'

'What's worse than what eats you?'

'Stop it. You said no messing.'

'You the one who said it.'

'Just stop it,' she said and she tugged on the belt loop.

'You just dreaming stuff up cause it's dark.'

'I don't wanna go no further.'

But he did not stop. He kept walking and she kept following, his arm reached forward and the lantern held in front. Pointing out when to duck an extended root or when there was a tricky step. They moved steadily and she would not let go of the belt loop and she kept asking him to stop, looking over her shoulder back toward the opening that had now disappeared. Stop, she said. But he moved on and she wasn't brave enough to turn around and be alone. The light of the lantern weakened as the flame burned the wick down toward its end and she yanked on his belt loop and slapped the back of his head and said you take me out of here right now. He turned and said damn you. Don't be slapping nobody.

'Listen,' she said. A quick command and she pulled her shoulders together as if getting ready to duck and hide.

'What?'

'Listen.'

There was the moan. Low and steady. 'I ain't doing this no more,' she said. She slapped him again across the shoulder.

But he did not answer her or acknowledge the slap. He held the lantern to the side and his eyes were ahead and into the black.

'Come on,' he said.

'I ain't going,' she said and her voice trembled now. Part anger and part panic. She pulled on his belt loop and said please.

He stared ahead.

'We can get out this way.'

'Stop playing.'

'Little bit further on.'

'Stop it,' she said. Crying now.

He began again and she moved with him. No other choice. The light nothing more than a spot of yellow now. Their shadows gone and the moan like some monotone song of hell. They were almost there.

The pit was right before them now. She slid her fingers from his belt loop and thought to turn and run but she was seized by the sadness that her life would never change. He knelt and set the lantern on the ground as the last of the wick burned away, a final flash of flame that gave them a brief glimpse of each other. His eyes alive and ravenous and her eyes watery and knowing. She wanted to cry out but there was only the black. The end of the world. Her nightmares alive now and she reached out to push him before he could grab hold of her but he had stepped to the side, and when she shoved and met nothing her momentum carried her forward and she stumbled and fell headfirst into the pit. Her final scream a piercing echo in the dark.

He stood there alone and listened and if she ever hit bottom it didn't make a sound. There was no thud or crying or calling. Only the silent thank you from the dark that now held him. He felt around and his hand found the lantern and he picked it up. Turned away from the pit and halfexpected a feeling of dread or regret or the necessity to repent but he only felt the fervent satisfaction of having done what he set out to do and before she was maybe even dead his thoughts were already turning to how he could feel this way again.

16

IN THE EVENINGS COLBURN WOULD come to the bar with his hair slicked back with sweat, flexing his hands from a day's work of hammering and bending and shaping. He would sit at the end of the bar away from the dozen or so after work regulars. Men with mud on their boots and women still wearing nametags. High schoolers shooting pool.

But today he was early and they were alone. The sunshine through the tinted glass door was the only somber light as Celia dumped ashtrays into the garbage and stacked beers in the cooler. Colburn sat and watched her, passing his bottle from hand to hand as if nervous and then he said I've seen it. Your house. You sitting out on the porch. And that blue hand lit up in the front window. She set the last of the beers down into the cooler and leaned against the bar.

'Why didn't you stop and sit with me?'

'I figured you were waiting on somebody who needed their future told.'

'I don't do it. It's something my mother used to do,' she said.

'Do you know the trick?'

'What trick?'

'You know. All the little tricks to figure out what to say.'

'She didn't think of it that way.'

'I figured a town like this would've burned her at the stake,' he said.

'You'd be surprised where people will look for answers when they think nobody's looking.'

'Can you do the trick?'

'I already told you. What she did wasn't a trick.'

'You know what I mean.'

'I don't know the answers to your questions.'

'That's not what I'm asking.'

'Then what are you asking?'

'I don't know.'

'I wish she was here. You could talk to her.'

'She wouldn't know the answers to my questions either.'

'She would try,' Celia said. Like she did with your father. She tried. She told me she tried. 'But you have to know what your questions are first.'

Colburn crossed his arms.

'How'd she die?'

'Just got older. Got sick.'

'Where's your father?'

'I don't know.'

'Did you ever leave here?'

'Two years at Ole Miss.'

'What happened?'

'For somebody who doesn't say shit about himself you got a lot of questions.'

He shook his head. Pushed his empty beer bottle toward her. She set another in front of him.

'It ain't for everybody. Besides my grandma and grandpa had a bait store in this building and they were getting ready to close it up. I talked them into letting me have it for the bar.'

'Bait?'

'And tackle.'

'I wondered what that smell was.'

'Funny,' she said. She disappeared through the swinging door behind the bar and returned holding a broom. She began sweeping behind the bar and Colburn got up and walked over to the jukebox.

'I heard you been walking around at night,' she said.

'Who told you that?'

'There's little eyes everywhere. What are you doing?'

'I don't sleep much.'

'You looking for something?'

He turned and looked at her.

'Like what?' he said.

She leaned the broom against the cooler. Took a rubber band from around her wrist and pulled her hair back and wrapped it in a ponytail. She picked up a cigarette pack from the bar and shook one out and held it between her fingers as she studied him. And then she said I might as well tell you before somebody else does. People know who you are. They know about your family. And they know ghost tales come to life because that's what your story is in Red Bluff. Nothing happens here, Colburn. Except for that one time when your father did what he did. I just want you to know that people know and I believe you when you say you came here for the free building but I believe you came for something else too. If you want to know what house, I'll show you. I don't mean to spook you but it's the truth.

He moved back to the barstool and sat down and said there

ain't a damn thing in this world you can do to spook me. And she started to tell him that his father had once and only once been in her house. Stood on the same porch where you saw me sitting. Your father sat in the front room of our house with my mother. Searching. One last time. He had been there and when we heard what happened my mother pulled the plug of the blue hand and she sat down on the floor with her back against the wall. Her eyes toward the ceiling. And when I asked her what was wrong she said he told me it was coming. I was supposed to be making up some bullshit for him, enough to keep him happy for another day or week or whatever they usually need but instead he told me his own future. He told me what was coming.

I can spook you, she thought.

But she didn't want to. She had seen it in the deep-set eyes of his hawkish face. She had seen it in the long stares at himself in the mirror behind the bar. She had seen it in the way his cheekbones rose when he wanted to ask a question that wouldn't come out. He's been spooked plenty, she thought. Don't do it. Not now.

It had been a quiet night. A few regulars in and out. And then Celia locked the door and turned off the lights over the pool table but she left on the beer signs and the room glowed in hues of red and blue. Colburn had been drinking and smoking through the evening and night, thinking about what she had told him but then he moved from that and tried to figure out what she was doing here. What anybody was doing here. There were moments during the day when there were signs of life, when people moved along the sidewalk or cars passed on the street or children cried or cash registers rang but something about it all seemed fake. As if this was not a real town but only somewhere people came for a few hours a day to pretend. A movie set where during the action there was life but after the scene was over and the working day had ended the town and its characters were forced to wait patiently until it was time to be used again. He had watched Celia and the way she moved with a flourish when she spun behind the bar or how she smiled at the regulars or how she sang along with the jukebox when she thought no one was listening. Her bare feet and twists of red hair and she held a vibrancy that seemed out of place.

After she had locked the door she came around and sat down on the barstool next to him in the hazy neon light and she said I like it like this. With just the glow against the dark. It feels like a dream. Like you can open that door and be anywhere you want to be. It's a dream and you are free to go and be and I sit like this sometimes all night. All by myself. But now you can sit with me. If you want to. I like it like this when it's late at night with just the weird light and the leftover smoke against the ceiling because it's strange. It's like a dream and it's always just my dream but if you want to you can stay here tonight and dream with me. I've never had anybody dream with me before. And if you want to you can even tell me what you're doing here. What you're really doing here.

He stood and walked over to the glass door. Stared out into the night. Moths circling the globe of a lamppost. A stray sniffing at a garbage can fallen on its side.

'I don't remember this place at all,' he said. 'I don't remember being here. Don't remember any kids from school. Don't remember the house. Nothing. How can strangers know more about it than me?'

'They don't know more about it. They imagine it. They make it up.'

'And we're a ghost story.'

'I wouldn't lie about something like that. I wouldn't have told you but I know what it's like around here. You would've either heard it from someone else or once everybody figured out who you are then they would have swallowed it instead. Looked at you like you were some kind of misfit. This place is one big ghost story. Stories about the valley. Stories about the man who killed himself. It's what we do.'

He crossed the barroom floor. Sat down next to her again. In the dreamlike haze he felt an honesty from her. Some kind of unexpected truth. Neither one of them spoke again for a long time. The only sounds were the movements of Celia trading out their beers or the rustle of a cigarette pack or the flick of a lighter. They sank together into the night and into the comradery of a pondering silence and then Celia got up from the barstool and stood next to him. Leaned her chest against his shoulder. Took the beer from his hand and set it on the bar. And then she slipped her arm under his and said come on. Come home with me. She expected him to say no but instead when she moved, he moved with her. She locked the bar and got in her car and he got in his truck. She drove ahead of him, waiting for his headlights to change direction but he followed her all the way home. But he did not say another word. Not as they walked up the steps and he stood behind her while she opened the front door. Not as they reached for each other in the darkness of the hallway, shuffling together into her bedroom and taking off clothes and falling into bed. She whispered good night to him later as they lay there in the dark but he did not answer. And when she woke up in the morning, he was not beside her but she found him standing in the backyard. Staring out at the valley.

17

MYER PUSHED AWAY FROM THE supper table. He tipped the bourbon bottle into the short glass and topped off his drink and then dropped in a couple more ice cubes before going outside. His rod and reel leaned against the wall in the carport and he grabbed it and walked down to the pond. He set the glass on a tree stump next to him. Rubbed at his knee which always hurt a little this time of day.

He cast across the pond. The lure hitting and sinking and the ripple reaching on and on in a growing circle. Gnats tapped on the water. Lightning bugs blinked in the twilight. Splotches of clouds sat in the low sky touched in the day's last colors. Through the open window over the kitchen sink he could hear the clinks and clatters of Hattie clearing the plates and washing dishes. He turned and looked at her. Her eyes down into the sink and her hands busy. Trails of her graying hair spilling from a messy bun and falling along her eyes and cheeks.

He picked up his drink.

She had told him when he became sheriff of this county that he would get fat and lazy. There won't be enough to do. You probably don't even need a gun. He had turned forty while they were moving into the house. A blond brick house with five acres and some trees and a little pond. This might as well be the end for you, she joked. You wanted a pond and got one. You wanted a fireplace and we got one. You wanted to be a sheriff and now you wear the star. Maybe I should start planning your retirement party.

He watched her in the window and she raised her head and caught him looking. Smiled. Wiped her hands on a dishcloth. He thought of her making fun of him on move-in day those twenty years ago. Thought of wrestling her to the floor, telling her to shut her mouth in the name of the law. Thought of how he let her win and she pinned him on his back and then how they knocked their naked bodies against the boxes stacked around them.

She was right, he thought. Mostly. He spent most days riding around. Checking on crews working on bridges or paving roads. Dragging roadkill off the highway. Eating fried chicken for lunch and sometimes for dinner. Maybe every now and then he had to run some teenagers off a piece of land they weren't supposed to be on. The only time he had even drawn his pistol was when he came upon a car slid off the road. Spinning its wheels in the ditch. He got out to see about it and a couple of deer sprang from the brush and darted across the road. Scared the shit right out of him and he snatched it as if being ambushed before misstepping and sliding down the slick incline and tearing his knees to shreds.

He took a drink and set it down again. Cast across the pond. The screen door slapped shut and Hattie joined him. She carried her own glass and the bottle and she sat on the stump. He reeled in the lure quickly. Cast again.

'What?' she said.

He looked at her. The dusk was coming on. The world turning vague.

'You always eat in a hurry and reel in a hurry when you're thinking about something. You've done the eating part.'

'You think you know everything.'

She smiled and sipped.

'Maybe I do,' she said.

'Maybe.'

He set the reel on the ground and picked up his drink. Walked a circle around the stump and said you remember my first week on the job. When I had to go over to that house. The woman was sitting on the front steps and her son was on the porch swing. Her face was so red and her eyes looked like something had been trying to claw them out even though she wasn't crying right then. Seemed to be taking a break from it. I remember she didn't say not a word when we pulled up and got out. She just raised her hand and pointed around the side of the house like she might've been showing us where to find a garbage can or the water hose. I sent my two fellas around back to the workshop but I stopped and talked to the mother and son. They nodded or shook their heads. I think the woman might have even gave me a full sentence at some point. But I'll never forget that neither one of them would look at me. Even when I tried to lean over and get in her line of sight she'd just shift her head and her eyes. Her son rocked back and forth on the swing. He was sitting on his hands and he never even so much as turned his head in my direction. I asked him his name and he never would say it. Finally his momma answered for him. Colburn, she said.

'Of course, I remember,' Hattie said. 'Why are you thinking about this now?'

He stopped pacing and stared across the pond and kept telling her all these things he had told her many times. I tried to say something nice but nobody knows what to say in a moment like that. But I tried. Then I walked around the house. My guys were standing in the yard. Smoking and looking at their feet. Neither one of them ever had to do anything like this either. The door to the workshop was open and we all three looked in right about the same time. I think some part of me expected him to still be struggling. Or swinging. I don't know why I thought I'd see movement. Because there wasn't any. Just a man at the end of his rope. One shoe had come off. Shirttail was out. His collar damp with sweat and spit and pink where a little blood had mixed in. Scrapes on his knuckles. His eyes half-open as if stealing one last look.

Myer finished the bourbon in his glass and poured a little more and did the same for her. She watched him, thinking I know all of this already. Why tonight? And then he said right then I smoked a cigarette. I don't know why I always remember that. It was like I didn't know what else to do so I smoked. One of my guys took some notes. Then they held him by the legs while I picked up a stool that had been knocked over. Grabbed a pair of hedge-clippers hanging from a nail. I climbed up on the stool and cut the rope and he folded over. They started to drag him out and lay him in the yard but I said God no. Leave him in here. They don't need to look back here and see him stretched out the way he is. So we laid him in the workshop and closed the door. Stood around and waited for the coroner. I looked up once and saw the son standing at the window, staring into the backyard. He was as unmoving as his father. I waved to him but he didn't wave back. I can't forget that part either. I couldn't imagine something looking as empty as that boy looked. I've laid awake many nights, thinking about the mother and the son. Wondering what they were wondering. Hoping they were talking to each other wherever they were because the day after they put him in the ground they were gone. I went over to their house to see about them and it was emptied out. She must've started packing about a minute after we took her husband away from there. I don't see how else it could've been done so quick.

Hattie listened. Something in his voice that blended with the dusk and the drinks that made it all seem new. As if he had cut the man down today and not twenty years earlier. She stood from the tree stump and walked over beside him. Waited. He rubbed his hand across his forehead and said a family has showed up in town. I think it's a family but I don't really know. Their car broke down. Hell they're pretty much broke down wherever they are. A man and a woman and a boy. I was gonna try to help them get their car fixed but they don't seem interested. And I guess I'm talking about all this because I never forgot how I felt when I stood there with the mother and son. Knowing what was in their backyard. Their eyes way off somewhere else. Damn near twenty years and I never felt like that again until now.

There's something about that man and woman and boy. It's almost like you can see them way down in a hole but know you can't do nothing to get them out. And if that was the only thing stirring around in my head then it wouldn't be so bad but that's not everything. You and me both know this place is dying. Has been for a long time which I can't complain about. It's kept me out of harm's way, which is pretty much all you can ask of this profession. But it's dying if not dead already. You know it's got so bad the town started giving away property right on Main Street. I guess they figured people here is better than no people here. There was a big story about it in the Jackson newspaper. Storefronts free for artists, musicians, whoever. All you gotta do is live here. Keep the place up. I don't guess it's such a bad idea but so far only one has showed up. When I saw the lights on in the building the other night I figured I might as well find out who it was so the next morning I went over to town hall. Asked to see the lease. Colburn, it said. I didn't even have to read the last name. I stopped right there.

Night had fallen around them as Myer talked. The pond a muddied blue mirror of the sky above. Nightbirds singing in sweet, love-song whistles. The windowlight from the house like eyes watching. Hattie rubbed her hand across his back. It's like when something moves in the dark, he said. You can't see it but you know it's there. I wonder if that's where we are.

18

CELIA HAD BEGUN FEEDING THE boy. Waiting outside of the bar and watching for him as he pushed the cart.

Alone now, she had noticed. No more of the woman trailing behind, waving and barking at him. The first day she offered she bought two plate lunches from the café. She ate hers with the door open so she could listen for the rattles. When he came along, she met him on the sidewalk. She held a cold bottle of Coke. When she said hello he ignored her and walked right past and then she asked if he was thirsty and she held the bottle out to him. He took it. Held it for a moment before turning it up and drinking in big gulps, the Coke fizzing in the corners of his mouth and streaming down his chin. He drank it all at once and then lowered the bottle from his mouth and let out a great belch. He gently set the bottle down in the cart.

She told him to come inside and eat. I got some leftovers if you want. But he hadn't accepted the first day. But on the second day he looked over her shoulder at the open door and then he walked over and peered into the shadows of the barroom. Then he stepped back out and pushed the cart away. Celia told him it would be there if he changed his mind and she walked inside and sat down at the bar. Counted the handful of receipts and the cash from the night before and then she heard the shopping cart again. She looked up and he stood in the doorway. The gangly silhouette of a dangling puppet. The Styrofoam container from the café was still on the bartop and she pushed it in his direction. Trying to lure a stray. She then opened the container and showed the mashed potatoes and gravy and porkchop and butterbeans and that did it. He came most days now and she wanted to ask him simple things. His name. His age. Where he came from. Where is that woman that used to follow you around. She would smoke a cigarette and watch him eat but she could never get to her questions because he ate with his face down to the plate and sometimes he used a fork but most of the time only his fingers, and as soon as he was done he hopped off the barstool and hurried out of the door as if she might somehow be able to take it all back before it could digest.

19

THE BOY KNELT OVER A pile of sticks and wadded newspaper. Working to get a fire started. A can of Vienna sausages and a straightened coat hanger on the ground next to him. One end of the back fender of the Cadillac dropped to the earth.

The man wandered into the hovel.

'Where's she at?' the boy asked.

The man paced. Rubbed at the back of his neck. He looked different. His eyes sunk deeper into their sockets, black dots surrounded by blood shot and void of color. His hair thin and tangled in filthy mats against his head. His lower jaw protruded more now and seemed intent on reaching up and swallowing his skeletal face. Its rough skin like a worn leather wrap of his cheekbones and forehead. His tongue and what remained of his bottom row of teeth worked together against his upper lip like some constant and hardworking machine and he had begun to tug at his earlobes to where they had become rubbery, little flaps that he reached for and pulled and twisted in an effort to manipulate the way the voices sounded in his head.

'Where's she at?' he asked again.

'Who?' the man said.

'She gone again?'

'I ain't been in there,' the man said.

'Huh?'

The man then looked at him. His eyes opened wide as if he had been surprised by the boy and then he jerked his head and cowered as if he were about to be struck by some judgmental hand. He moved his head in quick shakes and then he pulled at his own hair. He lips moved in silent conversation with himself and then he hurried out of the hovel and onto the road where he began a gangly run, looking over his shoulder as if being chased.

The boy pulled matches from his pocket. Then he stood and walked over to the Cadillac. Her clothes and pillow were still in the backseat. He opened the trunk and there were more of her clothes. Her coin purse. He closed the trunk.

He looked around the hovel. Down the slope where the world disappeared beneath the kudzu. He rubbed at his arm and tried to feel her next to him. Tried to remember what it was like when he was small and he would lie close to her at night. Sometimes her arm would fall across him. Sometimes she told a story. Sometimes there was a roof above them. Sometimes she told him it was going to be all right. But it had been a long time since any of that and he was left with flashes of memory like snaps of lightning that show you something beautiful for only an instant. He had listened to her crying since they left the little boy. In the middle of the night. Walking back and forth to town. Anytime when she thought no one was listening. And he had cried too as he lay across the backseat. Pretending to sleep after they told him what they had done and then drove out of the Delta, his face buried in his arms. His eyes squeezed shut. The thump of the highway a rhythmic reminder that they were getting farther and farther away and he would never see the little boy again. He had cried and nearly choked trying to hold it all in. Knowing the man would stop the car. Want to slap it out of him.

He didn't know why she wouldn't take any clothes. He didn't know why she wouldn't take him. He walked back to the pile of sticks and struck a match and lit the newspaper. As it burned he blew on the flames and the sticks caught and he piled on leaves and limbs and soon enough he had a good fire. He sat on the ground next to it and poked the little sausages onto the end of the coat hanger. Cooked them one by one and ate slowly. When he was done he lay back. He watched the firelight dance on the crisscross of the vines above and he wondered what the man had done to her.

20

THE MAN'S ARMS WERE POCKED with bug bites and scratched from crawling through the thorns and bristles and fierce kudzu vines and there was a taste in his mouth now, a steady sour that kept him spitting and dry mouthed. He sometimes disappeared into the tunnel for days at a time. Unaware if it was light or dark in the outside world. Sleeping and waking and at times confused over which was which.

He rarely ate. He rarely slept. A creature of the valley. The king of his own kingdom beneath the vines. He kept in a constant state of exploration, wondering if there were more secrets. More answers. Because that is what he believed he had discovered. His life until the moment he had begun to hear the voice just an open void of questions. Where we gonna get food and where we gonna sleep and why do I look like this and what brung me into this world and then stomped all over me. Questions that had exhausted him. Beaten him into defeat and acceptance. I didn't never need no goddamn teeth anyway he would think when another rotted and fell out. I didn't never need no goddamn place to sleep anyhow he would think when he fell asleep with his back against a brick wall. I didn't never need no goddamn body anyhow he would think the countless times when the woman told him she couldn't take this shit no more and then he wouldn't see her for a couple of days and she would then return. And then the boy. Jesus Christ a boy, he had thought when it cried and when it was hungry and when there had to be choices made over who ate what and the boy ate first and then her and then him. And then the boy getting big enough to walk on his own and then he was of use. A little more each year. He and the woman working together in whatever town they were in, a small one at her side conjuring up more sympathy and more reward at the back doors of restaurants and maybe a free night at a motel and then the boy getting to the age when it didn't work as well anymore. The three of them moving about this world in an unspoken language of grunts and nudges and handwaves. Keeping out of sight in shadows of alleys or in abandoned warehouses or within the woods. And then the other one was born. Jesus Christ another one. But he had gotten rid of the little one and he had gotten rid of her and he relished in the assurance that he was free to go as fucking crazy as he wanted to go. The voice spoke to him in the sweet influence of companionship. You are in the place you are supposed to be. This valley belongs to us and this is what I want you to do and this is how to do it. One answer after another and he felt solace in the peace that comes with knowing you have a purpose. Knowing you can affect this world.

The man was standing at the edge of the pit. Lighting matches and dropping them into the abyss. Listening to the moan and moaning along with it. He had moved to walk around the pit and venture deeper into the tunnel when the ground shifted and the earth slid and fell in crumbles. His feet were gone and he reached out for anything and his fingers dug into the ground and then one hand found a thick root and he grabbed hold just as he was about to go.

He hung there, grasping the root and one arm and one shoulder and his head above ground and the rest of his body dangling. The gravelly sound of the earth falling away. He grunted as he struggled and then gave a panicked wail, the sound echoing in the dark below and all around. He was not strong and could not hold for long so he began to swing his legs, gathering enough momentum to sling his other arm above ground, grasping the root now with both hands and his legs in a bicycle pedal as his feet searched for something to press against. But there was only the emptiness and he pulled and pulled, first his shoulders and chest rising above the pit and then his stomach and then he paused to catch his breath. Readying to throw a leg up. But then he felt the root give, a quick release and he saw himself gone before the root caught again. And he started over, afraid to pull too hard but having no choice, his grip weakening but fighting the pain in his hands and shoulders and he worked himself back up, throwing up a leg and planting a knee in the dirt and then feeling his weight rise from the pit as he collapsed on his side and rolled away.

He lay with his hands flat against his heaving chest, feeling his own heartbeat and trying to believe he was alive. Afraid of the earth collapsing again. Fearful of the demon hands that might reach up from the newfound depths and snatch him away. Distrustful of the comfort he had found in the dark and now suspecting that it had all been a trick. A lure. A sense of belonging meant only to prepare him to be devoured. And then as he lay there he felt a swell of fatigue. His body not wanting to move. His mind not wanting to make it. His muscles relaxed and he seemed to nestle into the earth. What else do you want, he thought. Then he sat up. He returned to the opening and he used the vines to climb out and into the light of day and as he wiped the dirt and panicked sweat from his eyes, he heard the twins for the first time.

21

CELIA STOOD IN THE KITCHEN. The sound of the radio and the crackle of bacon frying. Green tomatoes lay sliced on a plate next to the stove. When the bacon was crisp she laid the slices out on a paper towel and then she dipped the tomato slices in milk and then flour before setting them into the cast-iron pan with the hot bacon grease. Smoke and hisses came from the pan and she listened for Colburn. He had been walking through the house, calling out all he noticed that needed doing. A sagging strip of crown molding in the hallway. The paint flaking on the ceiling in the living room. All your windows need stripping and caulking. A couple of spindles are loose on the staircase rail. The floor needs leveling. The whole place needs a paint job. She told him to get started when he wanted but this is what an old house looks like. At least my old house.

She turned the tomatoes. Listened for his next suggestion. But he was quiet. She lifted the tomatoes from the pan and set them with the bacon. She waved a towel around at the smoke in the kitchen and clicked off the radio and then she stepped out into the hallway.

She found him in her mother's reading room, standing at the trunk with the lid open. A piece of paper in each hand.

'What is all this?' he asked.

'Stuff,' she said. 'Just stuff my mother wrote down.'

'It's all ripped up.'

'I know.'

She moved to him and took the strips of paper and she dropped them into the trunk and closed the lid.

'Come on,' she said. 'Let's eat.'

He ignored her and moved over to a bookshelf and he ran his finger along the spines.

'These are all over the place,' he said. He touched books on astrology, the occult, black magic, Eastern religions, voodoo, the saints.

'She was interested in lots of stuff.'

'Whatever they wanted to hear.'

'She wasn't like that.'

'Then what was she like?'

'She was a believer.'

'In what?'

'In possibility, I think? That there are other things out there we can't see or even know. Things that guide us and connect us. Save us.'

Colburn crossed the room and stood at the window. 'What about this valley?' he said.

'What about it?'

'You told me people say things about it.'

'Some people. There's stories about voices.'

'Voices?'

'Voices or songs or whatever coming from the valley. Mostly it's always been people who lived out here by it claiming such things.'

'Did your mother hear the voices?'

Yes, she started to say.

'I don't know. You'd have to ask her. Come on. I'm hungry.'

She grabbed his hand and pulled him along. Out of the room and down the hallway and into the kitchen. They sat down in high-back chairs at a table for two.

'There used to be a spring out there under all that,' she said. 'It twisted way down to the bottom. When we were kids we would go underneath and try to scare the hell out of each other. You can pretty much move underneath the vines if you know what you're doing. We found it then. I'll show you.'

'I'm not going under there.'

'Why not? You scared?'

'I'm an adult.'

'Same thing.'

The freckles of her cheeks and nose rose with her grin. She sipped from her coffee mug.

'There's other stuff,' she said.

'Like what?'

'A bunch of dogs disappeared in there. Not just old stray dogs that you see one day and not the next but it was dogs from town. Something would draw them out this way and they'd sniff about the edge of the kudzu and then wander in and that was it. Me and a couple of friends used to sit in chairs in the yard with some beer and watch. Here would come some dog trotting right alongside the road and then it'd go right in like somebody was calling it. Dog goes in. Dog never comes out. I bet I saw it happen three or four times.'

'I almost believe that,' he said.

'Maybe it was a killer dogcatcher living in that house under there.'

'What house?'

'Right about down in the bottom of the valley there's

this pretty wide hump with something straight sticking up. That's a house and chimney. My grandmother used to say sometimes you could see smoke still rising from the chimney if you looked out there the right time of day.'

Colburn shook his head. Cut a slice of green tomato and stuck it in his mouth. He chewed and gazed out of the window above the kitchen sink.

'What time of day are you supposed to look?' he asked.

'Around dark.'

'You mean twilight.'

'I suppose.'

'Everything looks smoky in twilight.'

'I'm just telling you.'

'You need to get out of here,' he said.

'Out of my house?'

'Not your house. This town.'

'How so?'

'You just need to get out of here. Go somewhere.'

'And do what?'

He didn't answer. And then she pointed at her head and said I'm so far gone already. I'm in a tent on the African savannah and I'm riding roller coasters built along the beach and I'm drinking hot rum sitting next to a fire with a white and frozen world all around me. Just because I'm here it doesn't mean I'm here. He grinned. Something in him wanting to steal her. To keep her for himself.

'Show me,' he said.

'Show you what?'

'The spring. The house down in the valley.'

'Don't make fun.'

'Then show me.'

'It's all grown up to get to the spring and the house is way the hell down in there.'

'Where was the spring?'

'You go in under the trees on the other side of the shed.'

'Come show me.'

'I'm eating.'

He put down his fork. Sipped coffee. Wiped his mouth with his napkin.

'I got to go anyway,' he said.

'Where?'

'There's only three places to go. Here or the bar or my building. I'm here now and the bar is locked.'

She laughed.

He stood from the table and then he leaned down and kissed her on the side of the head. Quick and awkward and she looked up almost surprised. He walked out of the back door and he paused to look at the shed. To look at the gathering of trees that stood behind it and the maul of vines that covered them. Then he walked around the house and climbed in the truck. But before he cranked it he reached into his pocket and took out the torn piece of notebook paper he had taken from the trunk. He unfolded it and read, making sure it said what he thought it said when he had heard Celia coming down the hall and he quickly tucked it away. The handwriting was sloppy and manic but it was legible enough and the words spoke to him from some deranged moment of time gone by, holding him now in breathless curiosity.

Somethins out there.

22

SUNDAY MORNING. MYER SCOOPED A cup of catfish food from the bag under the carport and then walked to the pond, the dew of the thick grass wetting the toes of his boots. He tossed the feed and the pellets scattered, little wet knocks on the surface of the water. He watched the ripples and waited. The smallmouths came first. Careful and grateful. But then the bigmouths appeared, their thick gray bodies rising from the bottom and pushing the smaller fish aside. Their mouths open and their tails slapping at the water as they twisted and turned. Myer squatted. Picked a blade of grass. Watched until the food was gone and the last of the catfish had sunk back down into the muddy depths.

'Myer,' Hattie called. She stood at the back door in a dress decorated with flowers on the shoulders. She held a casserole dish covered in tin foil and she stood with her hip propped out like she did when she was aggravated. 'Come on. We're gonna be late,' she said. 'And don't get your pants dirty. I just ironed them about five seconds ago.'

Myer stood. Looked down at his pants at the hard crease running down the front of the legs. He then set the cup on the ground. Tugged at his tie and pushed at his sleeves and he began back toward the carport where Hattie was sitting behind the wheel of the truck. He then reached inside the open window of the cruiser and took out his hat and put it on. She cranked the truck and he got in. The casserole dish on the bench seat between them.

'What'd you make?' he asked.

'Macaroni and cheese.'

'Didn't you make that last time?'

'As long as the church keeps wanting to have dinner-on-the-grounds every other Sunday I'll keep making macaroni and cheese. I claimed it and I'm sticking with it.'

She backed out of the carport and turned around in the yard. When she pulled into the road she asked him what he was doing wearing his hat. You never wear your uniform on Sunday.

'It's not my uniform,' he said.

'It's part of it.'

He took it off. Set it on top of the casserole dish.

'You don't want hat-head in church, do you?'

'I don't think Jesus would mind what my hair looks like as long as I'm sitting there.'

'You might be wrong.'

She smirked. Shook her head. They drove toward town. Tractors sat parked in fields in the tranquility of a Sunday rest.

Cows stood in shallow ponds anticipating the heat of day. The land rolled in emerald hills. The sky an endless reach of blue-white. Though she complained of being late Hattie drove casually as if the landscape was something new to the both of them. She hummed a hymn and swayed her head and Myer rode quietly. His arm propped on the door and his eyes lost in thought. The countryside slipped past and they came to town and bumped across the railroad tracks. Myer then perked up. Pointed and said take the next right.

'What for?'

'I want to go this way.'

'This ain't the way.'

'It can be.'

She turned right at a four-way stop and the street was lined with modest houses. Some with the carport on the right. Some with it on the left. The grass needed cutting here and there and barbecue grills and bicycles decorated the yards and lazy dogs raised their heads from porches and then slunk down again as the truck passed by. At the next stop sign Hattie asked him what now.

He leaned forward. Looked in both directions. Then he nodded forward and said one more block and then turn left. She studied him for a few seconds. Waiting on him to add something more. But he didn't and she drove on, following his directions. At the next stop sign she turned to the left and he told her to go slow.

'If I went any slower we'd be walking,' she said.

'Right there,' he said. 'Pull in right there.'

She turned into the one-car driveway. Shifted into park. The engine idled smoothly as they both stared at the empty house. The eyesore of the street.

'What are we doing here, Myer?'

Weeds and ant-beds owned the yard. The shrubbery grew in misshapen mobs of green. Vines of sumac had engulfed a porch column and reached up and fell across the roof. Rusted chains hung from the porch ceiling with no swing to hold. Plywood had been nailed across the windows and front door and the entire house wore the weathered and dingy look of the forgotten.

'Benny never could keep the house rented,' Myer started, ignoring her question. 'Somebody would move in and the neighbors or somebody else around town would tell them about what happened out there in the workshop. Then they'd hear every little bump in the night. Call me about it. Say they heard something.'

'I recall,' she said.

He picked up his hat. Turned it in his hands.

'I'd have to get up. Come over here and look around to make them happy but there was never anything to see or hear. Pretty soon the house would be empty again and Benny would find somebody to rent it again and then the same thing. Over and over. He finally quit on trying to rent it. Knew he didn't have a prayer to sell it. Told me he was going to let it sit here and let the badness leak out of it before he bothered with it anymore. Looks like it didn't work.'

'How do you let the badness leak out of a house?' she said.

'I don't know.'

'Who was the one who started calling it the house of fools?'

'I don't know that either. I guess it was a group effort. Some excuse to come over here and act like one. Then it was the neighbors calling all the time. Said they'd seen some kids over here in the backyard. Going in and out of the workshop and then finally locking themselves up in it and then running out squealing and hollering. Some scary game they had started to play. Soon enough the teenagers figured it out too. Except when they went inside the workshop and shut the door, they pulled beer out from under their shirts or coats. Thought it was real funny to sit in there and hide until somebody got buzzed enough to get panicked and haul ass.

It got to be pretty entertaining to go over there, knowing it was a handful of them sitting in there in the dark, sneak up on the workshop, and then just slap the hell out of the wall and listen to them squeal like pigs and then crawl over each other trying to get out.'

He set his hat down. Reached for the door handle but he didn't open the door. He shifted his eyes around to the side of the house. Imagined himself walking back there. Imagined what he was going to find. He crossed his arms and said the fun ended finally when a couple of them decided to go in the house instead. They broke in the back door. God knows how long that went on because when I finally caught two of them over there in stages of undress, the floor was littered with old beer cans and cigarette butts and condom wrappers. Benny damn near lost his mind when I told him about the condom wrappers. He stomped all over that house hollering about fornication and the devil's work and he swore that every sin that had happened inside those walls had descended straight from the crazy man who hung himself. I used to rent this house to families, he said. Sweet little families with sweet little babies. Now it's turned into a haunted whorehouse. I laughed. Told him that was a little strong. But his mind was made up and it wasn't a week before he had plywood nailed across the doors and windows. A lock and chain on the workshop door. NO TRESPASSING signs tacked to all sides of the house. I don't see them anymore though. Maybe people took them as souvenirs.

Hattie picked up his hat and the casserole dish and set them on the dashboard. She then slid across the bench seat closer to him. Touched her fingers to the sharp crease of his trousers.

'When's the last time you sat here?' she asked.

He rubbed his cleanshaven chin. Wrinkled his face in thought and said I wanted to make sure I remembered Colburn's name right so I pulled out the file. I was right. But I kept looking, trying to find something else I could say when I got ready to talk to him. Something besides you must be that boy all grown up. Something besides I came over and helped with your daddy. I looked for something interesting about the family but there wasn't anything. So then I figured I'd see what his life had been like, from the perspective of law and order anyway. And I wish I hadn't. He dropped out of high school right about the time he got arrested for petty theft. Then there was a whole list. Burglary, assault resulting in injury, resisting arrest, public intoxication, disorderly conduct. Most of them listed more than once. And the geography of it was all over the place. Arrests in Mobile, Hammond, Memphis, Hattiesburg, Jackson. He put together a pretty busy ten or so years but then the last five years have been quiet except for one simple assault. Some bar fight down in Vicksburg. He's a man now and I can go see him in the flesh and blood. But when I read his rap sheet all I could see was that boy, sitting right up there where that porch swing used to be. Looking at anything but me.

Myer pulled a cigarette pack from his shirt pocket. Tapped one out and held it in the corner of his mouth.

'You're not smoking in my truck,' she said.

'I'm familiar with the rules.'

'Can I ask you something?'

'Always.'

'Colburn. He done anything wrong since he's been here?'

'If he has, I don't know about it.'

'Maybe he just wants to see. Like you.'

'Maybe.'

She scooted back across the seat and nestled behind the wheel.

'We're late,' he said.

'Yep.'

'It's my fault.'

'Yep.'

'We're running out all your gas sitting here with it running.'

'I know a man I can get some money from.'

'Let's go then. He probably don't have as much as you think.'

Hattie shifted into reverse and backed out of the driveway. In the street, she paused. Both of them giving a long stare at the house of fools. Then she said you can smoke that cigarette if you want but only this time. He pulled the cigarette from his mouth and said I wouldn't dare break such a covenant. Especially on the Lord's day.

23

INSIDE THE REDBRICK CHURCH THEY were singing songs of resurrection. *Low in the grave he lay, Jesus my savior.* A full house. Women in white dresses and men wearing freshly pressed shirts. Little boys in tiny coats and clip-on bowties and little girls with shined white shoes and ribbons in their hair. Mothers and fathers and sisters and brothers and cousins pushed together into the same row. Hymnals open and mouths open in praise. *Waiting the coming day, Jesus my Lord.* In a room in the back of the church, behind the baptismal, the boy hid in the choir room closet. Listening. Their voices like something from heaven if he could imagine heaven. He squatted behind the hanging robes and leaned his head against the wall. Pacified by song and embraced by the soft crimson fabric of the choir robes, a gentle and foreign touch against his skin. He began to hum, trying to join in. *Up from the grave he arose, with a mighty triumph o'er His foes.* Inside they sang of resurrection and outside one had occurred. The man risen from the tunnel and prowling through the night. No sleep. The dark hours spent crossing the valley. Raising his head up between the vines to howl at the moon. The howl echoing across the valley until it was returned by some four-legged predator believing it was answering the call of another furred and fanged creature but this howl came from the slick-skinned and toothless. He had wandered all night and through daybreak and now he was outside perched in a tree on the church lawn. Wringing his hands and rubbing at his eyes in the constant movement of the anxious. *He arose a victor from the dark domain.* A long tent was erected on the church lawn. A line of tables down the middle covered with glass dishes and plates of biscuits and deviled eggs. Bowls of gravy and trays of chicken. Chairs and tables surrounded the tent and wooden crosses had been driven into the ground with mallets. A side door opened and the boy came out. He walked along the row of tables. Taking a piece of cornbread. Stuffing a deviled egg in his mouth. Sticking a chicken leg in his pocket. At the end of the table he picked up a bowl of potato salad and he looked over his shoulder, a quick glance to see if he was being watched. *And he lives forever with his saints to reign.* He then tucked the bowl under his arm and walked underneath the tree on his way to leave the church lawn and the man dropped down on him. A shriek as the man left the branch and crashed upon the boy. The bowl of potato salad tumbling to the ground and the man hanging on the boy's back, his arm squeezed around his throat and biting at the boy's ear with his slimy gums and the boy spun around. Trying to breathe and trying to break the man's arm loose from his neck. The man wrapped his legs around the boy's waist and held tight and then the boy staggered closer to the tree. His face red and losing his air and he began to slam backwards into the trunk, the man grunting with each blow as his back smashed against the tree, the boy ramming him again and again until the man let go and dropped to the ground. *He arose, he arose, hallelujah Christ arose.* The boy fell to his knees. Gasping for air. The potato salad beside him in the grass. He then reached over to pick up the glass bowl. The man had risen from the ground and was crouched, his long and dirty fingernails like claws and his crazed eyes and when he leapt for the boy, the boy clobbered him with the glass bowl, a resounding gong against the side of his mangy head. The man collapsed in the grass and did not move. The boy scooped two fistfuls of potato salad from the ground and dropped them into the bowl and then he ran. Inside, they held hands and prayed.

24

IT WASN'T EVEN A JAIL cell. It was a locked room in town hall next to the sheriff's office. There was a cot and a chair. The walls a dull yellow. The man lay on his back on the cot and Myer had waited long enough. He unlocked the door and walked over to the man and poked him in the ribs with the butt of a billy club.

The man snorted. Turned on his side. Myer poked him again and said wake up. You've been here long enough. The man opened his eyes and then sat up. He grimaced and raised his hand and touched the knot on the side of his head. Myer slid the chair over to the cot and sat down.

'It's time me and you have a good talk,' he said.

'I ain't ready,' the man said. He raised his hands over his head and stretched and then poked his index finger in the corner of one eye and scratched.

'You get ready.'

'Who put that knot on my head?'

'That's what I was about to ask you?'

'Don't figure how I'd know. Seems like that's the one you should be talking to.'

'I'm gonna be honest. I don't care about that knot or who did it.'

'Then why you got me sitting here?'

'Because I got up this morning and put on this shirt and tie you see me wearing. I went to church with my wife. Me and a whole bunch of other people. When we got done we came outside to have lunch and found you laying right there next to the food tables, knocked out cold. Besides that you smell like you been dipped in cow-shit and you're pretty much covered in a layer of dirt even dogs don't have. So I want to know what the hell is going on with you and your woman and boy.'

'I ain't seen no woman.'

Myer huffed. Stood up from the chair and walked over to the window. Outside the dogwoods bloomed, bright stabs of white against the rich green of June. Myer folded his arms and wiggled his nose against the rank smell of the man. He wanted to be on his porch drinking coffee and watching the hummingbirds dart to and from the feeder that hung next to the ferns. He wanted to be reading the newspaper. He wanted to have his feet propped up. He then turned back to the man and said it occurs to me I didn't start in the right place with you.

The man sucked at his gums. Shrugged.

'What's your name? That's the first thing I should've asked you in the parking lot. So let's go back to that.'

'It don't matter,' he said.

'Yeah,' Myer said. 'It does.'

The man turned his eyes to Myer and for an instant they seemed to come clear. As if he had just realized something about this world that no one else could know.

'People like you been wiping their feet on my name for long as I can remember,' he said.

'I've never done a thing to you.'

'It's the same face. You all got the same face.'

Myer hesitated. They are way down in a hole, he thought. And you can't get them out.

'Where's the woman and the boy?'

'I ain't seen no woman I said.'

'Then the boy?'

'Go ask him where he's at.'

'Enough of this bullshit,' Myer said. 'What's your damn name?'

The man's eyes fell to the floor. His lips moved but nothing came out.

'What?' Myer said.

'You leave me alone,' he said. 'I ain't done nothing to you.'

'Tell me your name in the morning or you'll be out there with the road crew filling potholes and we'll keep doing that every day until you decide to say it loud enough where I can hear it.'

The man stood from the cot and spit on the floor. He touched the knot on his head. He wiped his grimy hand across his grimy forehead. And then he said my name is Boucher. Now open this goddamn door and let me out of here.

25

THE COVERED HOUSE SAT IN the bottom of the valley. The hump of kudzu was broad and the chimney stuck up from its center like a green finger pointing to the sky. The boy had noticed it as he followed the road from town to the other side of the valley. Away from the hovel. Looking for a place to hide. Knowing he had to get away from the man.

He left the shopping cart on the side of the road and went beneath. His eyes watching for the man hiding behind tree trunks or waiting for him to leap up from a rain ditch. He wrestled his way through, unable to see the house but believing if he only continued down he would get there. And then thicker trees held the vines above his head and he was able to walk upright and he saw it.

The house was constructed in a crude rectangle. The planks of the short porch were warped in some places and rotted in others. The house sagged in the middle, the vines thick across the roof and trailing down its sides in strands of bondage. It had long ago been painted white but was now dulled with decades of grime. Slats from the woodframe hung loose and bunches of sumac and honeysuckle hugged the posts of the front porch like great green overcoats.

The boy stood at the edge of the porch. The front

door was open. Some window panes cracked and others missing. Vine and weed reached between the porch planks and wrapped the rails. He stepped onto the porch and the board gave with his weight but held and he took three more careful steps and then walked through the open doorway. A hallway separated the rooms down the middle, two on the right and two on the left. He looked from side to side, through the open doors of the front rooms. The walls spotted with mildew and mold and the floorplanks were spaced unevenly and vines slithered through. The floor was littered with dead leaves and broken window glass and chunks of plaster that had fallen from the walls and ceiling. The house mute with shadow and he breathed in the heavy scent of the organic world. His steps soft across the leaves and the floorboards speaking to him as he moved in small, cranky whispers.

The cracks in the plaster ran wild and crooked and the walls were stained from trails of rainwater that bled through the kudzu cover and into the crevices of the rotting roof. He moved to the end of the hallway and looked into each of the back rooms. One was the kitchen. A red stained cast-iron sink was set against one wall and a single vine spread across the counter and reached down into the drain. A cast-iron skillet and a kettle on the stovetop, each covered in cobwebs. In the middle of the room there was a round wooden table and one chair and beneath the chair there was a dark and deformed stain on the floor-planks that stretched out and reached beneath the table.

He turned from the kitchen and he stepped into the room across the hall when he saw the fireplace. Silvery streaks of water running down its sides and the bricks were streaked with black. The mortar cracked and fallen and the gaps between the bricks home to centipedes and beetles. The boy moved to the fireplace. Sat down on the edge. He listened, trying to figure out if he would be able to hear the man coming.

26

S ON OF A BITCH.

That's all Dixon could think of as he drove back and forth along the raggedy and winding road in front of Celia's house. Son of a bitch. He's in there. He had seen the flatbed parked beneath the pecan trees again and again as he made his way around the backroads that wrapped the valley and slipped through the countryside. Unable to sit at home and talk to Sadie. Nothing to say to her even though he believed he tried and nothing from her that made him want to stay. Eating supper and then saying I'm going out for a while and she didn't even ask where anymore. He just wiped his mouth and got in his truck and drove. Sipping from a flask of peppermint schnapps he kept tucked under the truck seat. Watching the sky fade into the color of gravestones as he drove to the package store at the county line. Getting a new half-pint and a quart of beer that he would sip on as the last light sunk down into the earth. The darkness settling on the world outside of him and inside of him.

These were his nights. He had chosen riding around instead of going to the bar since Colburn had arrived. He couldn't stomach the way Celia looked at him. The way Colburn sat at the end of the bar away from the others. The way they leaned to one another and spoke to one another in low voices. Like you got some goddamn secret that matters, he would think as he watched them. Leaning on his pool cue. His hands sweaty as he squeezed the smooth wood and watched them through the dull and dusty light. Son of a bitch. He had chosen the backroads now as a way to rid himself of the two of them and what he figured they were either already doing or would be doing soon enough. Her red hair pushed across her face and Colburn's hands across her bare freckled shoulders and the wild eyes of two people in the early days of discovery. Wild eyes he no longer saw as he looked in the rear-view mirror and wild eyes missing from Sadie's pallid face as she moved from one room of the house to another.

The flatbed truck was parked beside her car once more. Almost midnight. Lamplight in a front window and the rest of the house draped in shadow. The pecan trees standing guard in neat rows. He imagined wild eyes cutting through the dark in the room in the back of the house where he knew she slept.

Dixon passed the house and continued around the valley. The truck swerving between ditches and bumping over potholes new and old and when he reached the other side of the valley he stopped the truck on the roadside. He got out holding the quart of beer in one hand and the half-pint in the other. A halfmoon gave a dusting of ashen light and the valley rose and fell in shades of black. The kudzu like some web of the gods. He looked to the other side and spotted the space that belonged to Celia. The moonlight avoiding the dark house surrounded by dark land and dark trees as if giving Celia and Colburn the necessary solitude.

Their own vacancy from the spinning world.

He reached down and snapped off a piece of grass. Held it between his teeth. Something moved in the ditch and the weeds rustled with the nocturnal search for food. Dixon spit out the grass and took a long drink of the schnapps, draining the bottle and it burned good all the way through him. His eyes watering and he imagined raising his arms and spitting fire and then he threw the bottle where the thing searched about, a hard throw of frustration and there was a clunk of thick glass against critter skull. And then a moment of nothing. He waited for some little whine or cry. Some sound of struggle to survive. But there were only the wails of tree frogs and the rhythm of crickets and nothing more from the ditch. His aim dead on in the dark. When he couldn't see. When he had no chance. Maybe I'm doing it wrong, he thought. Maybe I should close my eyes and stumble around blind. Maybe that's how it works.

Why can't I stop thinking about it, he wondered. But he had no memories when Celia wasn't there. They had lived on the same street as children. Walking to school together. Sitting in the same classrooms. Playing together at recess. Walking home together and then climbing trees and riding bicycles and swimming at the swimming hole. And then becoming teenagers. Passing notes across the broad black table in biology lab. Eating lunch together and going to a Valentine's dance in the eighth grade and listening to records in her bedroom with the tall windows and she had never known how badly he wanted to kiss her. Or how when he was on the sidelines he was always looking into the sparse crowd in the bleachers to see if she was there. Or how he lay awake at night thinking about her during those teenage years and how he still did the same thing now. There had been those years when it went away. When he and Sadie were in the first years of being married and planting flowers in the flowerbed and painting the bedroom a different color. The years of trying to get pregnant and having a helluva good time until it instead became something of a chore. Something not working just right. And then she finally did get pregnant and though they were told it was a miracle they didn't think of it that way. They didn't think of it as a longshot so they planned like everybody else does. Having a shower and setting up a baby's room and ignoring what they both were thinking. Will we make it. And then not making it. No miracle.

He turned up the quart bottle and drank.

It was better that first time, he thought. At least I knew what the hell was going on. Because when it happened again three years later all she did was say I'm pregnant. And then two weeks later she said I'm not. And he had never been sure if she was telling the truth or only hoping and then they stopped talking about it altogether and now instead of being at home at night he went to the bar and shot pool and sometimes picked a fight. Years of this. Celia sitting again at the front his mind. The figure of something he couldn't have but he could sit on a barstool and watch her and talk to her and imagine his life in some other way and now Colburn had fucked that up and all he wanted was to get rid of him.

He pressed the heel of his hand against his forehead. He then pissed in the ditch. Lit a cigarette. He took one more look across the valley and then he climbed in the truck and drove again, lowriding deep into the night, the roads snaking around the valley and up and down the hills and he kept riding until he knew Sadie was long gone into whatever it was she dreamed of before he turned the truck toward home.

27

THE TWINS WERE IN THEIR backyard, in the space between their house and the kudzu. Both shirtless and one wore blue shorts and the other red. A clothesline ran between two iron poles in the shape of the letter T and they tossed a tennis ball back and forth, each holding a plastic cup and trying to catch the ball in the cup. There was a pause in the action as one of them stopped to tie his shoe and that's when they heard the rattling of the cart.

'What's that?' one said. The other shrugged. The rattling grew louder as the boy came along the road. The twins waited and listened.

'It's some old tractor,' one said.

'That ain't no tractor cause there ain't no engine.'

The rattling then stopped. The boy had made it to their pebble driveway and he was looking down into the garbage can when the twins came around the side. They paused at the edge of a row of azaleas that ran across the front of the house. The azaleas in full blooms of pink and white and the twins peeking between the blooms like curious birds nestled on a branch.

The boy bent down and his head disappeared into the garbage can that was rusted and pocked with dents.

'It's a old man,' one said.

The boy raised up holding two Pepsi bottles. He studied them for a moment, then looked up into the empty blue sky as if waiting on some type of affirmation and then he turned his eyes to the sun and squinted before he turned and set the bottles down into the shopping cart.

'It's a boy.'

'It's a old man.'

'No it ain't.'

They stepped out from behind the azaleas and crossed the yard. The boy was turning to reach into the garbage can again when he saw them. He stopped in motion. Half-bent. One arm extended. As if he were a sculptor's model.

'What you want?' one of them said.

They approached the boy and stood only a few steps away. One of them moved the tennis ball from hand to hand.

'Want nothing but this here,' the boy said.

'Goshdamn you sound like you fell down a hole.'

'Shut up,' the other said and he slapped his brother's arm. The twins then circled the boy and moved over to the cart.

There were green and brown and clear bottles. A piece of drainpipe. A strip of copper the length of a baseball bat. Aluminum cans and a nearly empty bag of chocolate chip cookies and a short stack of bricks.

The twins looked at one another.

'You want something to drink?' one said.

The boy nodded and then he waited while they ran inside together. The boy stood with his hands grasping the handle of the shopping cart as if someone might leap from the ditch and try to steal it away.

The twins returned with a glass of water and a hot dog. 'We got no more buns but we got this left over from lunch.'

'Momma said you could have it.'

The boy took the glass and the hot dog and nodded. He looked past them toward the house and their mother stood in the window but she stepped back when he saw her. He fed the hot dog into his mouth in one continuous motion of pushing and chewing and swallowing and it was gone.

'Goshdamn,' one of them said.

He drank the water in the same way, turning up the glass and drinking in thumping gulps as tiny streams ran down the sides of his mouth and made crooked lines across his pulsing throat. When he was done he lowered the glass and let out a series of heavy heaves as if having run a hard and fast race. One of the twins took the glass and set it on top of the mailbox as they watched him with marvel. As if he was a character from a Bible story or a comic book come to life, something they could only imagine before but now could lay their eyes and hands upon the real thing.

'You play ball?'

The boy looked at the ball and then the twins moved back from each other and tossed the tennis ball back and forth.

'Come on,' one said.

The boy stepped from the roadside and into the thick grass. He did not know how to stand or what to do so he watched and waited until the ball was thrown his way and then he raised his hands and slapped it away as if it were an enemy.

'Don't fight it,' one of them said.

'Let it come to you and just catch it. It ain't hard.'

The boy picked the ball up from the ground. He gave more of a push than a throw and the ball fell weakly between the twins.

'Not like that,' one of them said as he picked it up. 'Like this.'

He made a slow-motion movement of throwing while the other narrated. Don't squeeze the ball so tight. Pull your arm back. Bring it forward and let go at the top. Follow through and let your arm swing on down after you let go.

The ball came back to the boy and he fought it again but the ball bounced off his hands and against his chin and he cradled it, trapping the ball against his collarbone. His expression shifted into something of satisfaction as he looked up at the twins and one of them clapped in approval.

'Now throw it like we showed you.'

The boy squeezed the ball. But not too tightly. And then he drew back his arm and he had started to bring it forward when a thwack came from the edge of the valley. Somewhere beneath. The twins both looked out across the side of the yard, where the sound had come from. They moved toward it and stood at the edge of the kudzu. Waiting for another sound or some movement.

'Tree probably cracked and fell,' one said.

'Probably,' the other answered.

The boy stood there in the yard. He looked at the twins and then he turned and looked all around. Squeezing the tennis ball now. His eyes shifting around and he saw the mother in the window again and this time she waved. He lifted the tennis ball to her. The twins came back into the yard and said go on and throw it. The boy began again, drawing back his arm but then he stopped. His head turned in a jerk and he looked out into the kudzu as if being summoned.

'What?'

'You see something?'

The boy only dropped the ball on the ground. He moved between them, walking in the direction of the sound. The boys stood still and the mother stood still in the window.

'It ain't nothing.'

But the boy continued to drift across the yard and toward the valley. And then there was another thwack and the boy stopped.

'It ain't nothing,' one of them said again.

The boy wiped his hands on his pants as if getting ready to grab hold of something. The twins began walking toward him but when they were right behind him he suddenly turned around and they leapt back.

'Goshdamn,' one of them said. 'Don't do that shit.'

The boy then lowered his eyes to the ground and walked across the yard in the familiar sullen gait he used when not wanting to be seen. When he wanted the eyes of the world to stop looking at him the way they looked at him. He crossed the yard and he took the glass from atop the mailbox and set it down into the shopping cart and he started pushing it along the road. They asked him to stop. Told him you ain't got to leave. But he kept on and he ignored them and they stood in the yard and waited until the rattle faded away.

28

COLBURN STOOD AT THE FRONT door of Celia's house. Late afternoon. She was at the bar and he knew because he had ridden by there to make sure and now he was second-guessing himself. Don't go in there, he thought. Not without her. But he did anyway.

He had never seen her use house keys and he didn't expect the door to be locked. It wasn't. He walked in and left the door open behind him. He went to the trunk. Pulled a chair next to it and sat down and opened the lid. Somewhere in there was his father's name and a note from his visit. He had seen enough of the scraps to realize the pieces of paper were not only torn ramblings but records of who came and went.

He searched with both hands. Picking out the torn pages as if participating in a game of chance at some morbid carnival. A game that was rigged. A game that you could only lose no matter how hard you tried. He found names and he found dates and he found more incoherence but he could not find what he was after and the trunk seemed to have no bottom. Endless fragments from her psychic world. He leaned back in the chair and huffed. Stared up at the ceiling fan.

Then he got up and went into the hallway and he opened the only closed door.

It was her mother's bedroom. A cast-iron headrail for the

bed and the covers were rustled. A cobweb wrapped around the small chandelier hanging from the ceiling. A massive armoire stood against one wall with its doors open and clothes were on the shelves. Not in neat and folded stacks but instead in wads as if thrown toward the armoire from the other side of the room. A half-dozen open boxes were on the floor and some held framed photographs and cups and dishes. Some held underwear and socks. Some were empty. Nails stuck out of the walls where the frames had been.

Next to the bed was a gramophone and Colburn sat down on the edge of the bed and stared at it. As a boy he had danced in the kitchen with his mom when Elvis came on the radio and he liked the way she moved in fits of happiness when his voice filled the air. And he had sat in the hallway of their new house in a new town and listened to her cry through the door of her bedroom in the weeks following the death of his father as she played 'Love Me Tender' over and over and over on the gramophone until he came home from school one day and found the gramophone in the garbage can next to the mailbox post.

He had taken the gramophone from the garbage can and carried it into the kitchen and plugged it in. The table turned and a static hiss came from the horn. The horn elbow was slightly bent and he gently forced it back into position. There seemed to be nothing wrong with it and so he poured himself a glass of water from the faucet. Her footsteps coming from the hallway and then stopping when she came into the kitchen and saw it there. Put it back in the garbage. I don't want to see that thing again. He explained that it still worked and that he had straightened the horn and she picked it up and raised it over her head and slammed it down on the linoleum floor.

A crash and fragments bouncing into the air and shooting across the floor. I said throw it in the damn garbage can and I mean it.

He said yes ma'am and he carried out the big pieces and swept up the small pieces and the garbage truck came by that evening and the gramophone was gone. He had been sitting on the concrete steps of the front porch and he heard the truck coming from one street over and then it turned the corner and he watched it move from house to house and as it came closer he felt the rise of fear inside his small chest and he believed there to be something else in that garbage can that would go away and never come back. He sat and watched and crossed his arms over his chest and squeezed as if he could somehow hold on to whatever it was he could not name and the truck stopped and the man stood down from the back and waved to him. Feeling it all as the man raised the garbage can and dumped it into the back with the rest of the trash and then he looked at the boy once more before he slapped the back of the truck and the engine heaved and the truck moved on to the next house.

And that was when she began to disappear. No more dancing in the kitchen and the random meal on the table and a growing depth behind her eyes like some great eroding crater where wind and rain came steady to carry life away. Him growing into a bigger boy and then a teenager and she did not notice and she left the back door open for him to come and go as he pleased and sometimes in the spring or in the changing colors of fall she would come around for a little while. Her eyes and her smile and a pan of biscuits for breakfast and asking about his homework and then just as he settled with her being his mother again she would retreat into the black as if hiding from an intruder. And then from the dark she emerged on a cold December day and she came to him as he sat alone in the kitchen. He sat alone eating a bologna sandwich and studying the guide for his driver's test and she had come into the kitchen and sat down at the table with him. Her eyes on the salt and pepper shakers in the middle of the table and he watched her and waited. He had learned to wait on her and not ask any questions or make any moves and let her come to him. She finally raised her eyes as the cold winter air came underneath the space below the back door and seeped between the edges of the window frames and her eyes were shadowed and tired and she looked at him with her head bent to the side as if looking for someone else and she said your brother would have been nineteen years old today.

And he said, what brother?

A car door slammed in front of Celia's house and Colburn jumped. Moved his head in a quick shake to break free from memory. He stepped out of the bedroom quickly, closing the door behind him. He then moved to the open front door and looked out and he saw the cruiser and the tall man with the badge pulling himself out of it, grimacing and grabbing at his back as he got upright. Colburn stepped out onto the porch and down the stairs and Myer came toward him. The men stopped in the high grass of the yard and looked at one another.

'I had figured on saying hello to you under more cordial circumstances but since we're standing in this spot, I'll just ask what are you doing out here?'

'Just stopping by,' Colburn said.

'This ain't your place.'

'I know it.'

'Then what are you stopping by for?'

'Nothing. Just seeing if she was here. That against the law?'

'You know Celia?'

'Yeah. Do you?'

'Everybody knows Celia.'

'Then ask her.'

'What am I supposed to ask her?'

'Ask her if she gives a damn if I stop by.'

Myer scanned the place. Listened for movement inside. 'You alone?'

'Yeah.'

'I recognized your truck.'

'Recognized it from what?'

'From being in town. Parked out in front of your building. You make a pretty good rattle riding around with all that scrap tied down.'

Colburn nodded. Took a few steps to walk back toward the flatbed.

'Hold on,' Myer said.

Colburn stopped. He had been here before. Within arm's length of some kind of law. With the caution and the voice telling him to hold still and he never liked it before and he didn't like it now. He looked Myer over. The gray stubble and the sharp eyes and the lines of time carved around their edges.

'You don't mind waiting while I go in and look?'

'It's nice of you to ask even though I know you're not really asking.'

'Then wait right here.'

Myer passed close to him, their shoulders nearly touching.

'You all think you know something but you don't,' Colburn said when Myer was past him and up on the porch.

'What'd you say?'

Colburn kept his back to him. He pulled a pack of cigarettes from his pocket.

'I said I'll be right here waiting, sheriff.'

Myer stared at the back of Colburn's head. Then he moved again and he went inside the house. Colburn lit a cigarette. The windows were open and he watched Myer move from room to room. His figure dark through the screens. Doors opened and closed while Colburn smoked and listened to Myer's boot heels knock against the hardwood and he was leaning on the grille of the flatbed when Myer came back out and down the steps.

'How you enjoying town?'

'It's fine. It's free.'

'Ain't such a bad deal. You ever been here before?'

'Nope.'

'That right?'

'That's right,' Colburn said and he moved toward the truck door.

'Colburn,' Myer said.

Colburn paused. Flicked away his cigarette.

'Your name is on the building lease,' Myer said.

'Okay,' he said and he reached for the door handle.

'I've been here a while. About twenty years.'

'Good for you.'

'I've been meaning to stop by the building. See what you're up to.'

Colburn dropped his hand from the door handle. Turned to Myer.

'I get the feeling there's something else you want to say besides what you're saying.'

'Only to tell you I was there,' Myer said. 'Last time I saw you, you were sitting on the porch with your mother. It's been a long time. I was just surprised when I saw your name.'

'I don't really care about all that.'

'You need anything?' Myer asked.

'Like what?'

'It's just something I thought I'd ask.'

'Why don't you go ahead and say it?'

'Say what?'

'You looked me up. I can see it in your eyes. Hear it in your voice. You're not keeping me standing here because I was some sad little boy who broke your heart.'

'I just want you to tell me the truth whenever I ask it.'

'Like when?'

'Like when I ask you if you ever been here before.' Colburn huffed. Laughed a little. Lit another cigarette. 'The truth, huh? That's what you want?'

'That's right.'

'Your truth or mine?'

'I didn't know there was a difference.'

'I figured you wouldn't.'

Myer shook his head. Scratched at his chin.

'We'll try this again sometime,' he said. 'You can go.' Colburn opened the truck door and climbed in. He cranked the truck and shifted into drive, making a big circle into the yard and then weaving between the pecan trees before turning onto the road. He looked over his shoulder and Myer was watching him drive away and he stomped the gas and drove harder. The two miles into town disappearing in an instant and his head filled with the thoughts of his mother and his father as he pulled into the parking lot of the bar and he stomped the brakes and the flatbed skidded to a stop. From the sidewalk someone yelled out for him to slow his ass down but he did not hear them and he did not see where he was or what he was doing and he shifted into park and sat there with it all.

29

WHAT BROTHER?
Your father always meant to fix the fence, his mother said. She was wrapped in her bathrobe and wearing a vacant expression as if not knowing who or where she was. She and Colburn sitting together at the kitchen table. Every day he meant to fix it but he never got around to it. He'd hear that dog barking in the middle of the night and he'd roll over and mumble I got to fix the fence as if he was talking to himself in a dream. Or we'd be drinking coffee on the porch and the dog would stick its head through the gap over behind the bushes and he'd say I'm gonna get it fixed this weekend but he never did. Jacob wasn't but two years old. That was your brother's name. Jacob. Your father had picked it out. He wasn't but two, almost three in another month or so. But that fence. Between our house and the neighbor. Had a gap in it big enough for that dog's head to start with but I guess it just kept on pushing and pushing until it could get its whole body through. It had already come in our yard a few times and your father had run it off. And it was a mean dog. I remember when your father tried to scare it away it didn't do nothing but look at him. Didn't jump or scatter like most dogs will do when you stomp at them. It was a mean dog, had eyes that would look right through you. Like it was already thinking

about what it would do to you if it had the chance. Its face was tight, seemed like the coat was pulled back so far it might just tear off. And its coat was gray like a storm cloud except for this white streak right between its eyes. I never trusted it and I told your father that and he said he was going to fix the fence. Every day he said it. But he never did.

She shifted in the chair. Stared at the tabletop. Colburn had begun to feel nauseated while she spoke as if falling from a great height that offered no safety below.

It had already killed, she said. Dragged up this other dog one day. Didn't nobody even know where it came from. It just came walking up the street dragging this dead dog. Held it by the throat, clamped down in its jaw. That dog walked up and down the street holding the dead dog by the throat like it was showing off some trophy. Like it wanted to prove to everybody what it could do. Your father went over there then. Told the man he better do something about his dog before something really bad happened and the man didn't argue but I don't know how he could have anyway. He tied it up for a little while in his backyard. It actually took a real chain that dog was so strong. And I remember the ping of the man driving an old railroad spike down into the ground to hold the chain and hold the dog. It was fine for a while and we stopped thinking about it and I guess your father stopped thinking about the fence but some way or another the dog ended up wrestling itself free and wandering around again. So we wouldn't never let your brother anywhere outside unless it was in our yard cause we had the fence. But the fence still had the gap at one of the posts and your father kept saying he was going to fix it. I don't know why he never got around to it. I still can't figure out who to blame.

Her eyes seemed to retreat further back into her head as if sliding out of existence. Outside the clouds had covered the sun of the cold December day and a muted light filled the kitchen and gave the feel of an old photograph. As if she were some image of the past that could not be reconciled or manipulated. Colburn listened to his mother but it seemed as if she wasn't his mother but only wore the skin of the woman he had known. As if her confession of this previous life was a final transformation. Into what he didn't know.

Her hair was tucked in a loose bun on the back of her head and she had taken her fingers and twisted several of the stray strands. She sniffed. Took a deep breath. And then she said it was my fault because I knew better than to let him out there alone. I just didn't think nothing of it and I don't know how you're supposed to be able to imagine something like it happening. How your mind is supposed to go that far. It was a hot day and we had all the doors and windows open. Fans blowing. I was doing something. I don't even remember what. And Jacob kept pushing at the screen door and hollering to go out so I flipped the latch and let him go out there. I swear I didn't think nothing of it. You don't think about stuff like that. Your father had run down to the store and right about the time he came in the front door we heard it happen and I remember we looked at each other right at the second we heard it and we both knew before we could even get out into the yard. We both just knew like it was something that had been planned since the beginning of time. Maybe it had.

She folded her arms on the table and she laid her head down to the side. Her eyes filled with trepidation as she saw it all again and her breaths began to skip. Colburn did not move. Did not speak. It replayed in her mind and she watched

it and heard it and her mouth parted in the same terror as it
had so long ago when they had run into the backyard.

What brother? he thought.

This brother.

She raised herself up and said I don't know why we decided
to never tell you about him. It was your father's idea. It was
his idea to leave town and start over somewhere new and we
didn't figure we'd ever have another child. Didn't neither of
us want to. I think we both thought we could run away from
what all happened. Like it was some bad story we'd heard
somebody else tell.

She then replayed their arguments in her mind but she did
not tell Colburn what his father had said when she told him
she was pregnant. Four years after it had happened. Four
years gone and neither talking about it. Only going through
the motions of a life. She did not tell and would never tell
her younger son that his father said no. You aren't having it.
I don't want it and I'll never want it. We'll go somewhere and
get it taken care of. I want it, she had told him. I don't care if
you do or not. I ain't going nowhere to get that done, not to
our baby. It won't be our baby, he answered. It'll be your baby.
And she had said you don't mean that but he did mean it and
though she had believed it was a sentiment that time would
wear away he had never acted any differently than the way
he promised he was going to act. That child will live in my
house and I will provide but my son and my only son is dead
and I killed him because I didn't fix the goddamn fence and I
won't be a father to another child in this lifetime. I'll take you
to get it done if you change your mind and you better think
on it. I ain't thinking on it, she had said. And I hate you for
even saying it. Hate me then, he said. And he would walk the

floors at night as she lay in bed with her belly growing and imagining this child as a vessel of recovery but she listened to him pacing in the hallway and talking to himself. He prayed to God that God was bluffing. That this wasn't really happening and can't you do something about it and I won't love it and I don't care what you do to me cause you done enough already. I can't believe you would do this to us again. Pacing on the hardwood floors in his sockfeet not wanting to wake her but talking to God without censor about the child he did not want and would not love and she lay there and listened and tried to close her eyes and sleep. Lying on her back and her hands on her belly and whispering to the child. Don't listen to him. He don't mean it. Please don't listen. Her hands on her belly where she thought the child's ears might be. Don't listen to him. Please don't. He will love you and so will I. She had swallowed all of this down, never speaking a word of his father's resentment to another soul, hiding it below the surface of living in hopes that some miracle of love would somehow find its way into their lives.

What did you do about it? Colburn asked.

About what?

The dog.

Oh.

A dishtowel lay on the table and she picked it up and dabbed at her eyes and then she said I don't even know if your father had ever shot a gun before. But he went and got a shotgun and a box of shells from somewhere and then he went over to the dog who was back on the chain and he shot it until it was nothing but a puddle. He shot it so many times and for so long the people in the neighborhood came out of their houses and wandered over to see what was going on.

A crowd stood around and watched while he shot the dog again and again and some of the women cried and I don't know if they were crying for the dog or for your brother or some of it all. If I remember right a policeman even pulled up and he only got out and watched with everybody else. That man who owned the dog stood there with his arms folded. Leaning against a tree in his backyard. He didn't say nothing and when your father had shot the dog to the point where it couldn't be shot no more he raised the shotgun and held it on the man. I was watching over the fence and I wanted to tell him to do it. I wanted to scream it. Kill him. Please just kill him. And me and everybody else thought he was about to except for maybe the man who never moved. Kept his arms folded and kept his shoulder leaned against the tree and he just looked at your father like he wouldn't blame him. But then your father lowered the barrel and he knelt down on one knee. He propped the butt of the shotgun on the ground and he turned the barrel around toward his own face and he put his mouth around the end of it like he was trying to swallow the whole thing. And nobody moved. Not that man and not the policeman and not nobody else who had come to see what was happening. It was like time came to a stop. He stretched his hand down to the trigger and held his finger on it and I closed my eyes and waited for the sound of the rest of my life falling apart. But it didn't. Not then anyhow. I opened my eyes again and he had taken the barrel from his mouth and he tossed the shotgun on the ground and he stood up and walked off down the street and I didn't see him until the next day. I don't know why we never told you. It was an awful idea and I'm sorry because I think your life and your father's life might have been different if we had.

She passed the dishtowel from one hand to the other and then she laid it out flat on the table and smoothed it.

Even at fourteen he understood. He understood the indifference and the disinterest and the feeling that he was nothing more than a bother to his father. The questions he asked that his father would not answer and the pleading to go with him when he walked out the door and his father ignoring him and cranking the car and leaving him standing on the front porch waving his small hand. He understood the silence of the house and the deep set eyes of his father and the way they had always looked right through him as if he was only a shadow, some useless silhouette. I do not love you and I do not want you he had heard his father say a thousand times with the way his father glared at him when he did something wrong or when the boy tried to tell him about something that happened at school or when the boy touched him on the shoulder to tell him good night. I do not love you and I do not want you and he understood it now that his mother had admitted the grief they both had sucked down and digested for his entire lifetime and he saw his father's sunken face when there was quiet in the workshop and he heard his father's voice when he told him to get the hell out of here and he saw his father hanging from the beam of the workshop. He understood that he had been right in the moments when he wondered if he had done something to him. If he had committed some unforgivable sin. And he had.

He had been born.

His mother reached across the table and held out her hand to him. I'm sorry, Colburn.

But he did not take it. And he did not answer. He was fourteen years old and with her hand reaching out to him in a feeble gesture of apology he began to calculate how much longer he had to live in that house. He looked at the study guide for the driver's test that was still in his hands and he did not see pages filled with the correct answers to the questions but he saw instead the possibility of leaving. Of having the legal right to get into a car and drive away from her and away from here and away from the photographs of his father that hung on the wall and away from the simulated life they had all lived together. He looked again at her empty hand and it was the hand of a stranger. Not the hand of a mother and not the hand of a friend and not the hand of comfort and though she had given birth to him against the wrath of his father she had not loved the way she should have loved. She did not fight the way she should have fought. And he understood and she had wanted him to forgive but in that instant he set his eyes toward the day when he would leave her to deal with it on her own. To sit alone and wonder if he gave a damn. Just like they had done to him.

30

COLBURN SAT SLUMPED IN THE truck seat and stared vacantly at the steering wheel. And then he mindlessly opened the door and wandered across the parking lot as if punch-drunk from the past and he pulled open the door to the bar and stood at the threshold. Inside along the bar sat a plump woman who had just come from the beauty parlor with her mountain of hair. Next to her sat three men still wearing their orange roadcrew vests. Two men with loosened tie knots shot pool and a humpbacked man with a cane whacked at the cigarette machine trying to get an extra pack to fall out.

'Quit doing that, Ed,' Celia called to him. She was behind the bar pulling fifths of liquor from a box. 'You do that every time.'

'One time it's gonna work.'

'If it does you can't keep them anyway. Anything extra falls out of that machine, it's what we call house cigarettes.'

Ed gave it another whack and then took the pack he'd bought from the tray. He ambled over to the pool table to watch.

Colburn stood in the open doorway. The rectangle of light behind him and his face dark and they all squinted in his direction.

'Close the damn door,' one of them said.

He took a step inside and the glass door fell shut behind him. He walked over to the end of the bar. No one spoke to him and he didn't speak to anybody. Celia pulled a beer bottle from the cooler. Popped the top and set it down in front of him. A strand of hair fell across his eyes and she reached over and brushed it away from his face. She touched his arm but he remained trancelike.

'Colburn?' she said.

And then the word came from one of the men with pool sticks. Because he had been waiting for a chance.

'Freak,' Dixon said. The hard-sounding word carried clearly across the bar room and right behind it were short and uncomfortable laughs. Celia turned around and saw him leaning against the pool table, his face bent in disdain.

'Shut up, Dixon,' Celia said.

'Yeah, Dixon. Shut up,' another voice sang mockingly. More laughter. Dixon tugged at his tie that was a little too short. Tugged at the belt of his pants that were a little too tight. He gave a sneaky grin of satisfaction to the regulars and then dropped it as he saw Celia staring at him.

Colburn let out a deep breath and then seemed to awaken. His eyes fresh as if only now seeing where he was and when Celia turned back to him and asked if he was all right, he nodded and picked up the beer and drank.

'I'm going to my building,' he said.

'Don't let the door hit you in the ass,' Dixon cried out.

'I told you to shut up,' Celia said.

'Come with me.'

'I can't right now,' she said.

He leaned closer to her and lowered his voice and said I don't want to be in here. I want to be with you somewhere.

And she whispered back to him. Just sit down for a little while. Drink your beer. Smoke my cigarettes.

He nodded. Sat down on the empty stool next to him and the pool game restarted. The regulars began to talk to each other again. The knocks of bottles against the bartop and the flicks of cigarette lighters. Colburn drank the first beer quickly. Celia gave him another and he was turning the bottle in his hands mindlessly when the cue ball jumped from the pool table and bounced across the floor, rolling to a stop at his feet. He bent down and picked it up and Dixon was coming around to his end of the bar to retrieve it.

When he reached Colburn he held out his hand. Colburn stood. Walked to the door and opened it and he took one step outside and slung the cue ball down the street. Then he came back in and sat down again. He picked up his beer and took a swallow that he didn't finish before Dixon gave him a hard shove with both hands and knocked him clear from his stool. The beer bottle launching from his hand and his feet flying up and his arms reaching and grabbing at nothing and he landed flat on his back, the air going out of him in one big bounce and the bottle clanking and spinning across the floor. Celia came across the bar and snatched Dixon by the arm as he was moving toward Colburn and when he shoved her aside, two of the men in orange vests rose from their barstools and hugged Dixon and dragged him toward the door. Because that's what Celia was yelling for them to do. Get that son of a bitch out of here.

She followed them outside and when the two men turned Dixon loose she said you better just get in your damn truck and go home. His shirt had come untucked and he'd lost a button as the two men wrestled him out of the door. He was breathing hard as the men walked back inside the bar and left them there together in the muggy afternoon.

'You need to stop it,' Celia said.

He unknotted his tie. Slipped it from around his neck and stuck it in his pocket.

'You hear me?' she said.

'He ain't hurt.'

'I know he's not hurt and that's not what I mean and you know it. You've got to stop being such a lunatic every time somebody decides to sit close to me.'

He huffed. Looked down at the ground like a scolded child.

'Are you listening?'

'I'm standing right here and you and me both know I can hear you.'

'I didn't say do you hear me. I said are you listening to me.'

'It's not every time,' he said.

'It happened with Coney and it happened with Lamar Johnson. Both times right in there by the pool table. Keep trying to pick a fight until they can't take it no more and there you have it. Just like today. And I've been watching you.'

'Watching me what?'

'I've been watching how you watch Colburn when he's in the bar. How you watch when me and him are sitting there talking. You got to stop and I mean it. This ain't high school no more, Dixon. That's long gone.'

He wiped a line of sweat from his upper lip. Pursed his lips and shook his head. Knowing she was right. Knowing he'd acted a fool. Knowing he would again.

'He don't belong here and he don't belong with you,' he said.

'You're being stupid,' she said.

'It ain't stupid. There's something that ain't right about him. I don't give a shit what happened to his daddy and what he's doing back here.'

She stepped toward him and then walked a frustrated circle before she said go on. Go the hell home or wherever it is you're going but just go and don't come back over here if you're gonna start shit up with Colburn again. Or if you're gonna start shit up with me or anybody else. Because if you do it again then you can find another place to drink your beer and shoot your pool.

'There's not anywhere else.'

'Then you'd better pull it together.'

Colburn had gotten to his feet. Picked up the beer bottle and taken a towel from the bar and wiped up the spill. And now he watched Celia and Dixon through the glass door. Behind him somebody said I guess we can't play no more pool. Somebody else said if I was you I wouldn't bother coming in here no more when Dixon is around. Another voice said maybe he's right about you.

Colburn then turned around. All eyes were on him. 'Right about me how?' he said.

No one replied.

'Right about me how? Goddamn say it,' he yelled. But they would not answer. Bottles raised to mouths. Cigarettes to lips.

He reached over the bar-top and down into the cooler and he grabbed two beers and walked past them. Glaring at the backs of their heads as he moved behind the row of stools. Staring back at the humpbacked man with the cane who leaned against the pool table. Kicking the storage door open and moving past the cases of beer and bottles of liquor and throwing open the back door and then finding the boy digging through the garbage. Picking out aluminum cans and putting them into a burlap potato sack.

'Get the hell out of here,' he said.

The boy was leaned over with his arm down into the bin. He raised up and looked at Colburn with tired and unaffected eyes.

'I said get the fuck out of here,' Colburn yelled and then he heard his own name called. A shout from behind. And he turned to look though he knew who it had come from and Celia stood in the opening of the back door. Her eyes past him and to the boy who was backing away with his sack of cans, little tin rattles with each careful step.

A flush of shame washed over him and he looked back at the boy. Pocks of dried blood along his arms from scratching bug bites and wearing two different shoes. One much too large and his toes sticking out of a hole in the front of the other. Colburn had always thought him a boy when he had sat there with Celia and watched him eat, but as he looked at him now he saw something different. Neither boy nor man but something in between. A sloping back and the calculated movement of those unsure or unconcerned. Colburn moved over to the garbage bin and dug out three more cans and hustled to catch up with the boy, who was easing along the side of the bar building. Colburn opened the sack and stuffed the cans inside. He pulled three dollars from his pocket and gave them to the boy.

Then he came back to Celia. She was leaning in the doorway with her arms folded, her brow crooked with the annoyances of man. He walked over and stood right in front of her and her eyes fell on him and he said when you get done come out to your house as soon as you can. Don't ask me why. Just come on. I'm gonna build a fire and wait. There are things I want to tell you that I've never told anyone else and that might keep you from coming. And I wouldn't blame you if it did. But I wish you would think about it. I'll be there.

31

COLBURN GATHERED FALLEN LIMBS FROM the pecan trees and piled them behind the house. He took bricks from the side of the shed and formed a loose circle down the slope of the backyard only steps away from where the kudzu began. He had gone into the shed and found a hand saw and he trimmed the branches from the limbs and then sawed the limbs too thick to snap over his knee. Working in the twilight and sweating with the back and forth of the saw and feeling better with his heart thumping harder and the satisfaction of doing something.

Soon enough he had a fire going and he had taken two aluminum lawn chairs from the back porch and moved them next to the pit. The young fire snapped and hissed and he sat with his legs crossed. His hands folded on top of his knee. A reverent pose as he waited for Celia.

It was almost midnight when she arrived and she came sauntering across the backyard in silhouette and she held a bottle of wine gripped by the neck in each hand. She sat down next to him and gave him the bottle that was already opened and set the other on the ground and said we are probably the only people in this whole countryside sitting by a fire tonight. Celia uncorked a bottle and they passed it back and forth.

'I should probably tell you about Dixon,' she said.

'I don't want to know anything about him.'

'If somebody shoved me off a barstool I'd want to know about him.'

'Well. I don't.'

'What do you want to know about?'

'Nothing right now.'

'Then why don't you do the telling then? That's why I came out here. Because of what you said. Because of the way you said it.'

He moved then. Shifted in the chair. He set the bottle on the ground and looked at her with the firelight shifting on her face and making curly shadows from her curly hair and she said you can tell me. And he didn't want to be like his parents anymore. Keeping it all hidden behind years of strained eyes and forced smiles, sucking their grief down into a poisoned silence that could only spread and ruin. She squeezed his arm and said whatever it is, you can let it out.

He told of his father's swollen face and bulging eyes and his empty mother and the story of a brother he never knew. The brutality of indifference and the years of his wasted boyhood trying to please a man who could not be pleased and the years of his youth he had wasted trying to figure out what he had done to put the noose around his neck. The hand of his mother held out to him when she told him about his brother. As if such a simple gesture could erase a lifetime of questions and guilt and how he had left her hand there to lie on the table. Open and empty.

Then he circled back around to the moment he had gone toward the workshop. The silence as he approached and the anxiety of opening the door and having to see his father's snarl and hear his bark but he went on anyway like he had been told to do. And I remember thinking maybe this time would be different. Something inside of me always thought the next time might be different. But I opened the door and he was struggling and he waved at me with one hand and seemed like he was tugging at the noose with the other. His damn mouth was foaming and his toes were barely touching the top of the stool and then he started reaching up, trying to get hold of the banister above his head but the rope was too long and he couldn't reach it. I want to say I was hollering or crying but I wasn't doing either. I should have. I know I should have. But I wasn't.

The entire time Colburn had been talking he had been pressing his open hands together. Harder and harder. His hands beginning to shake a little with the pressure and Celia wrapped her own hands around his. The tension releasing from his hands and forearms as something seemed to drain from him. But then he filled back up again as he took her hands and moved them away and said that's not the end of it.

I think he wanted down. I think he changed his mind. I guess people do that when they walk up to death. I guess they decide maybe things aren't as bad as they seem. Maybe I could do better. Maybe I can fix whatever needs fixing. I watched him and he kept waving his hand around. For what I don't know but then I decided to help him out. To help us both. If he wanted up there then that's what he was going to get. He didn't care nothing about me and he was never going to and I would rather he hated my guts than acted like I wasn't alive and that came on me stronger in that moment than it ever had. I had never been nothing but invisible to him and now all of a sudden he could see me with his toes tapping on top of the stool and his air going out. I didn't know why I should help him. Even if that's what he wanted.

Colburn's face had changed. His features stark in the firelight and his eyes brazen and staring down into the flames. Celia touched her fingertips to his lips to try and stop him from talking anymore but he wrapped his hand around her fingers and held them close to his mouth. I did what I did, he said. It didn't take but one hard kick to knock the stool over. And that was that.

32

CELIA WAITED FOR HIM TO say something else but he was done, sitting there slack and heavy-eyed. The fire was dying down and something screeched across the valley. She stood and said come on. Let's go inside. She held out her hand and when he didn't take it she tugged on his shirtsleeve. Come on, Colburn. It's late.

'I have to go,' he said.

'I know. That's what I'm saying.'

'Not from this spot. From this place. From this town. I need to get away from here. I should have never come back in the first place.'

She sat down again.

'There's something wrong with it,' he said.

'With what?'

'With this place.'

'Did all that really happen?' she asked. Her voice filled with the kind inquisition of already knowing the answer.

He got up from the chair and walked to the edge of the kudzu. He reached down and picked a leaf from the vine. Held it at arm's length as if it were a mirror. Then he let it fall from his hand and he turned to her.

'Come with me,' he said.

'Come with you where?'

'I don't know. It doesn't matter. You don't have to stay here anymore than I do.'

She stood and moved next to him. The fire down to ember and a red glow against their skin. How could you never tell anyone about this, she wanted to say. How could you hold it for so long. What part of you kept it hidden. Where will it go now. You look broken and you are broken and it's okay to be broken.

'This is my home.'

'There's no such thing.'

'For some people there is.'

'Well. It's not mine.'

Celia backed away from him. Walked back to the chair and picked up the bottle of wine. She drank some. Listened to the night. Drank some more.

'Have you gone over to your old house?' she said.

'I told you the night I met you I didn't know which one it was.'

'Do you want me to take you?'

'No.'

'Isn't that why you came here? To see it?'

'Yes. Maybe.'

'Then I can show you.'

'No.'

She drank again. Didn't know what to say. Thinking now of how often she had caught him in a dead stare. His eyes hard and void of emotion. Snap out of it, she would say before when she caught him. Realizing now it was not so simple, that in those moments when he stared at the sky or at the wall or at a spot on the floor he was the child again. He was alone in a house with other people. He was lifting his foot to kick away the stool. He was leaving the shed and walking into the kitchen to tell his mother she needed to come outside and he was standing alone in the backyard listening to her scream as she moved inside the shadows and greeted the dead. She moved back to him and touched his arm.

'When I look out the window of my building, I almost expect to see myself walking along the sidewalk,' he said. 'Dragging his body along behind me.'

He stood rigid and she wondered how much he was like his father. If something had transferred from one soul to the next in that moment in the workshop. And then she wondered about being here with him now. If it was like the conversation her mother and his father had shared so many years ago, as the blue neon hand shined and the incense burned as her mother was pushed back by his father's darkness. By his promise of what was to come. No smalltown psychic bullshit. No token promises of the bill collector staying away or the husband getting sober or the ghost of a dead grandmother hovering in the corner but something different. The customer instead telling her about his life in ways her mother hadn't been prepared for. I had nothing for him, her mother had told her years later.

Nothing to take him off his path. Nothing to make him feel better. Celia held her hand on Colburn's arm, standing in this flat circle of time that held them both and she imagined that one day a child with her blood and a child with his blood would find themselves on the edge of this valley, under the same moon and stars and sharing the same nightmares. Time coming around again.

He did not respond to her touch. She sat down and lit a cigarette and set the bottle of wine between her legs. Colburn then walked around the fire and he picked up the other chair and moved it closer to her. She gave him a cigarette. And then he said while I waited on you out here I went looking for your spring. It's still there. I found a machete in the shed and I cut a little path. It's a nice spot. She leaned her head over against his shoulder. He touched one of her curls. They sat quietly then, listening to the crickets singing. An owl calling. Two orange dots of their cigarettes waving around in the black like fireflies. Two eyes from somewhere deep in the darkwood watching them.

33

THE BOY HAD MADE THE vine-covered house in the belly of the valley his own. In the back room with the fireplace he prepared a bed of leaves to sleep on. In the corner he kept the odds and ends he swiped from Colburn's building when he wasn't there and the small pieces of Celia he took when she wasn't looking. A hairbrush. A napkin she had doodled on. A rubber band she took from her wrist and laid on the bar. He used Colburn's chisel to carve stick figures into the plaster walls. Creating others to be there with him that could not speak and had no eyes. He cleared the vines from the hallway and from the door to the porch steps. A pathway across the warped planks that gave a welcome.

In the night he sat on the edge of the fireplace and struck matches and burned small piles of twigs and leaves. The chimney filled with vines and the smoke pushing out of the flue and filling the room. Some part of him was always listening for footsteps. Listening for the smacking of his lips and gums. He pretended that the vines would protect him. That if the man came close to the house or even made it into the hallway the vines would grab him by the ankles and wrists and drag him away while he wrestled and cried and then the boy felt the vines coming for him. An intrusion into their world. Sliding into the house and sliding along the hallway and then bending into the room where he slept. The air changing and blowing strangely cool and the croaks and chirps pausing and he would sit up. Wave his hands around his head as if to shoo them away and if that didn't work he would get up and move over to the wall and press his hands against the stick figures as if they were there to protect and he imagined his hands in their hands and the smooth-skinned touch of a loving embrace that was alien to him.

On other nights he sensed the man. His black-humped figure creeping. His patient steps creaking across the floor. The smacking of his lips. His hard eyes and the darkness draping him and his hands covered in blood. The boy would hold the chisel in one hand and a long-handle screwdriver in the other and sit in the corner with his heels pressed against the floor and his back pressed into the corner as if to try and shove himself into some other realm. Clutching the weapons with sweating palms and short breaths of fear and the night moves of the man and whatever evils he brought along with him and maybe dragging the woman by the hair, her slack body leaving a trail of the dead. Sometimes he heard the little boy crying. Faint and helpless in the distant dark. Out of reach. The boy's body gripped in tension and his eyes alive in the dark and waiting and waiting for something to leap at him or grab at him and then finally he would hear the first birdcalls and he knew that morning was near. That he had survived. That when the light seeped down below the kudzu and the dull blue entered the house, he would once again be alone.

He made one more trip back to the hovel. He took what was his from the Cadillac and piled it in the shopping cart. Then he turned the key and shifted the car into neutral. He released the emergency brake and hopped out and watched the Cadillac roll down the slope, gaining speed enough to crush the brush and skinny trees that held up the vines. He watched and listened to the cracks of limbs and crunch of leaves as it rolled away and then the vines collapsed and tightened around the Cadillac. Held it stationary. Swallowed it. And he felt something of his life disappear. Remembering the four of them in the car. The little boy lying across his lap in the backseat. The man driving and smoking and sometimes singing a little song. The woman with her hair flapping in the wind and her eyes still able to see a better day.

34

COLBURN DROVE ALONG THE FAR side of the valley. He
stopped when he noticed a roll of barbed wire and a pile
of fenceposts next to a mailbox. He got out of the truck and a
sprawling magnolia tree stood next to the wood-frame house,
the large limbs shaking and he heard the voices and then the
twin boys emerged through the slick green leaves.

'Hey,' Colburn said. 'Your momma home?'

'She's sleeping,' one of them said.

'Her head hurts,' the other one said.

'What about your daddy?'

'He ain't been here for a long time.'

'Oh,' Colburn said. 'How old are y'all?'

'Ten,' they said together.

'Old enough to tell me about this stuff here?' Colburn said
and he pointed at the barbed wire and fenceposts.

'What you wanna know?'

'You throwing it away?'

'I guess so,' one of them said. 'It was just old fence that ran
around behind our house between us and the vines.'

'Uncle Billy did it,' the other said.

'Looks like it's set out for the garbage man.'

'Looks like it.'

'Can I take it?'

They looked at one another. And shrugged at one another at the same instant as if they had counted it off.

'Yes sir,' one of them said.

'Tell your momma I said thanks.'

'She don't care,' one of them said. 'She hated that old fence.'

The boys watched as Colburn loaded the roll and the posts onto the back of the flatbed and they were still watching as he drove away, his cigarette hand hanging out of the window.

When he was gone they returned to the tree and climbed up and down the thick magnolia branches. And then they tossed the tennis ball back and forth over the clothesline. Then they sprayed one another with the garden hose and when one of them yelled the other said don't wake up momma. You know how she gets. Then they raced laps around the house, each winning two and then calling it a draw instead of racing a tiebreaker. A thick cloud moved across the sky and blotted out the high sun and they walked away from the house to where the kudzu began, covering a low-rising bluff they could climb by using the vines as ropes. Standing on the bluff and looking up at the span of the stone-gray cloud and then playing the game they always played in the kudzu, across a hillside where smothered azaleas and blackberry bushes held up the green tapestry and provided space to move beneath. One walked up the hillside and then sank down into the green leaves and disappeared while the other waited on the bluff.

'Marco,' he called.

'Polo,' the brother called back from beneath the kudzu. The boys had learned to crawl and slide without rustling the leaves. Without giving themselves away. Covert children in a shaded world. The first brother moved from the bluff and called out again.

'Marco.'

'Polo,' the other brother called back from a slightly different spot.

'You got to say it louder than that.'

'Just play.'

The twin moved up the hillside and to his right, in the direction he thought his brother's voice came from.

'Marco.'

'Polo.'

And then a rustle. A movement that gave the hider away. 'You might as well give up. I see you.'

The twin moved on toward the spot where the leaves had moved. A green hump up and then down.

'Marco,' he called.

He waited but there was no response. He took a few steps deeper into the kudzu.

'Marco.'

A low rumble of thunder from the ever gathering clouds above. The boy crept with high steps as if trying to navigate across a field of mud.

'Marco, I said. You're cheating just like you always do. I already see where you are so just go ahead and answer,' he said and he moved on toward the spot.

'Marco!' he yelled. 'Either answer me or I ain't playing no more.' The kudzu waisthigh now and the sky going gray and the feeling of being alone that he had not felt before in his young life. His own image always there beside him.

'Come on. Quit messing around.'

Then from behind him another rustle. He turned his head

to look but never saw where it came from as his feet went out from under him and his chest and head and flailing arms disappeared beneath as if he had jumped into a deep body of water. And when the mother woke later from the gusts of an afternoon storm, she would call out for the boys and when there was no answer she would walk to the back door and look out into the rain and across the hillside. Call out for them again. The wet, green cover and the waving leaves and a great and empty void only beginning to open inside of her.

35

A STRAIGHT AND STEADY RAIN began to fall the day after the twins disappeared, the vines growing thicker and greener with each drop. Myer and his deputies and deputies from neighboring counties met in the parking lot of the Baptist church at daybreak each morning and volunteers joined them to form the search parties. Myer would divvy the numbers into several groups and each group approached the valley from a different side and then they all tromped and tripped across the valley, aggravated by the rain and the dogs getting tangled in the vines and the rain making the leaves slick and shiny and the footing beneath slick and slippery.

Red Bluff had gone from being nowhere to being somewhere in only hours. The fear and heartbreak had awakened the sleepy town with gut punches of emotion and the television crews that came and the reporters who asked questions to whoever they could get to talk on the sidewalk and the police and detectives who moved in and out of the café and post office and gas stations in their white shirts and black ties were all symbolic and clear in their message – we would not be here unless tragedy has befallen. A constant stir among the townspeople. What happened and how did it happen and I wonder if they've figured out anything and lock your doors and watch your children.

They read about it in the newspaper. Heard about it on the radio. Talked about it during Sunday school and at the counter in the café. No one knowing anything and as the days went by without answers, the stories began to form. The suggestions of a greater evil lurking about in the depths of the valley. The suggestions of worlds unknown beneath the kudzu where man or woman or child could disappear. Suggestions that were shot down by those who sat within earshot with their children or who wanted no part of the supernatural when there were real hands who had done the real snatching and that's what the hell we got to find.

Myer could not fight the vines with his lanky frame and the tweaks in his back so he would observe from the roadside above the valley, aggravated at having to watch the younger and stronger men. He held an umbrella and watched throughout the morning. An investigator would stop by and they would talk or a reporter would stop by and Myer wouldn't talk. He paced around the cruiser and waited for the radio to call him and say we got them. Or we got something. Any goddamn thing would do but there was no such call. At noon the men would climb out and eat sandwiches that the café had made up for the search parties. There were only bits of conversation as they ate and then smoked as the rain fell on them and they stared out across the kudzu with their expressions a little longer each passing day. Time moving on. Not one shred of evidence. The battle being lost to the mangle of the vines.

In the afternoons he began his own search. Driving the countryside and stopping at abandoned houses or trailers. Going inside and opening closets and moldy refrigerators and deepfreezes and then crawling underneath and swatting away spiderwebs and shining his flashlight. Calling for the twins and getting aggravated by animals nested in the crawl spaces, their movements making Myer's heart thump with hope that it was the twins and not some hairy four-legged thing. He would crawl out and then have to bend and stretch before he climbed back into the cruiser and drove again. Going down skinny dirt roads he hadn't been down before, the trees thick and reaching over the roads and the feeling of driving through a green and shadowed tunnel. He came upon barns that were barely standing, crippled by time and the weather. He climbed over and around stacks of haybales whose ties had dry-rotted and the hay fell slumped like melting snowmen and he kicked away snakes and looked into horse stalls and climbed broken ladders into lofts but there were no twins and when he called out for them his voice fell dead in these deserted worlds.

At night he would stand out by the pond behind his house still wearing his wide brim hat, the rain tapping against it. The rain tapping against the brown water of the pond. The rain tapping like some finger on his shoulder in a steady reminder of their inability to find the twins. Hattie would call to him from the cover of the back porch. Come in, Myer. Come sit up here with me. But he would pace around the pond, the heels of his boots sticking in the soft ground of the banks and the rain still falling and the clouds pushing down against the earth in a thick gray cover. He would finally cross the yard and sit down with her on the porch. Take off his hat and shake it. Take off his coat and shake it. She would have the bottle and a glass sitting there waiting for him and he would pour himself a short drink. She asked if there was anything new and sometimes he made up something to give himself optimism and other times he only shook his head. She would leave him and he would drink another short pour and then another and finally go inside. He did not sleep in the bed but instead he lay on the floor. The stress triggering the pain in his back and the hardwood floor a better spot, lying there flat with his knees up, listening to Hattie sleep and watching the rain trail down the bedroom windows.

36

COLBURN HAD BEEN QUESTIONED BOTH by Myer and by state detectives in the first days after the disappearance because he had been the last to see the boys alive. He explained he had seen the roll of barbed wire and pile of posts next to their mailbox. He explained they came down out of the magnolia tree, just two boys doing what two boys do on a late afternoon. No I didn't see anyone else. No I didn't see the mother. No I didn't see anyone else on the road. No they didn't act like anything was wrong. I loaded up and left them standing there and that was it. They then asked him about his hands that were bruised and scratched and he explained that they stayed that way from his metal workings and digging through scrap piles. He explained his hands and then two days later had to explain his hands again to another investigator and then they didn't ask him any more questions but he was stuck with a tag he did not want to be stuck with.

The last to see them alive.

The phrase had stuck in Colburn's mind like a fragment of some gruesome poem and he began to repeat it in his head in rhythm with his steps when he walked. He began to repeat it as he swung the ball peen hammer to flatten or bend metal and steel. The last to see them alive. How many goddamn times in my life, he wondered. Sometimes he whispered it as he drove around the countryside. Sometimes he said it to himself in the mirror after he brushed his teeth. He had begun to feel the eyes of the locals upon him as he walked down the street or sat in the bar. No longer because of what his father had done and the stories that had been concocted about his family. But because they all knew he was the last to see the twins alive and late at night before he fell asleep he had to fight back the guilt seeping into him, the strange notion of having participated in some way.

The moment the rain stopped he was standing at the edge of the valley behind Celia's house. Two weeks gone since he had talked to the boys in their front yard. It was the middle of an afternoon. The sunlight streaked through the diminishing clouds and the air turned thick and heavy. Within minutes the steam was rising, seeping up between the leaves, wisps of exhaust that rose and formed a cloud that settled over the silent land.

I don't believe in ghosts, he whispered. He then took a step to walk back toward the truck and he thought he heard a whisper. *Come here.* He stopped and whirled around as if to catch himself in some strange act of self-manipulation but there was only the mist. The blades of light cutting through the clouds. And a valley grown deeper and stronger with the blessings of the rain.

37

THE BOY NOTICED THAT SOMETHING was going on and he tried to stay out of the valley. He did not go down to the covered house until late at night and he barely slept and was gone again before the morning gray, when he heard the yapping of the dogs like some canine alarm. He had found a place to hide himself on a bluff that rose above the twins' house. A curtain of vines falling across the ridge and he sat behind the vines and he spied on the men going in and out of the house. He recognized Myer and he recognized Colburn as they several times stood next to the mailbox with other men and Colburn pointed and explained.

He was nearly asleep hidden on the bluff on the night when the church bus stopped on the road in front of the twins' house. A great exhaust when the engine turned off and then the door folded open and a crowd of men and women and children moved in a broken line around the side of the house and across the yard and they stopped at the edge of the valley. Formed a half-circle. A woman moved around with a box and each person took a candle from it. Then a man in a white robe faced the valley and raised his hands and raised his voice and as if Mother Nature was paying attention, the rain began to ease while he spoke and then it paused. The man in the robe then lit a candle at one end of the half-circle and one by one they passed the flame until the candlelight glowed in a dim crescent. There was a quiet moment as the man in the robe moved his hand over the head of each of them and when he was finished they began to sing. Their voices reverent and angelic. A sweet prayer across the valley for the safety and the return of those who had been lost. They sang and the women held the hands of the children and the man in the white robe knelt at the edge of the kudzu, his hands pressed together and his head bowed and their voices joined in solemn song. Kind and aching.

The boy had been sitting with his legs crossed but when they began to sing he rose to his feet. Moved by their tenderness. Moved by their plea and by the candlelight and by the children participating in the sorrow. The boy stepped onto the edge of the bluff and when the man in the white robe rose from his knees and lifted his hands above his head the boy did the same thing. Raising his hands slowly toward the night sky and moving his fingers as if to grasp something just out of reach and then in his ancient voice he tried to hum along with the prayerful hymn and in this moment of joining in he looked over toward the house and he saw the flatbed truck and Colburn standing in the side yard. Solitary and shadowed. His arms folded and watching them. The boy lowered his arms and he began to wave them from side to side, as if his movement could shove Colburn toward the gathering. They sang and prayed and the candles burned but Colburn remained apart and when they were done they blew out their candles and set them on the ground and then they walked back toward the bus. Colburn still there but none of them speaking to him or looking at him but for one small girl who raised her hand and waved.

After the bus was gone, Colburn drove away. The boy came down from the bluff and tromped across the kudzu and into the backyard. He picked up a candle that had been stuck into the ground as a remaining beacon. He took a pack of matches from his pocket and he lit the wick and then he stood there with the solitary flame as if he himself could be the salvation to what had caused the agony.

38

THEY LAY TOGETHER IN CELIA's bed. The middle of the night. A breeze through the open window and in the distance a train horn echoed in the dark. Colburn had awakened. Thought he heard his name. And then he realized where he was and his eyes adjusted to the shadows. He lay on his back. His eyes wide open. Celia lay with her back to him and he rested his hand on the curve of her hip. Felt her breathing.

He moved his hand from her hip and he sat up. When he woke in the night there was no going back to sleep and he wondered how much longer until morning. If daybreak was close enough to make coffee and sit on the porch and wait for the sunrise or if there were hours yet to suffer. Hours to tolerate in the dark and envy those who slept. The clock was on her bedside table but he didn't want to look. He could feel it. The long dark ahead.

He lay back down. And then she whispered. Surprising him.

'Have you ever been married?'

'No. Have you?'

'Do you have your own child somewhere?'

'No.'

'Do you have anyone anywhere?'

'No.'

She then turned over and faced him. Her hands beneath her head on the pillow. The sheet fallen from her and the moonlight brushing the skin of her shoulders. He waited for her to say something else but she didn't and when he looked at her, her eyes were closed. He wondered if she was talking to him in a dream or if she was talking to him at all or if there was someone else behind her eyes that she needed to ask these questions.

He was careful not to move. Her rhythmic breathing resumed and she seemed deep into the dream-world and he wanted to be in there with her. Believing her dreams were not like his but protected. She had whispered to him and now he began to whisper back. His eyes to the ceiling. I feel something taking hold, he said. I don't know what. I always wondered if there was one person like you. Someone to just be there with. But I wish we could run. Celia moved. One hand sliding from beneath her head and moving to her side. He did not look at her because he was afraid her eyes were open and he wanted to finish. I don't want to stay here, he whispered. Something is not right. I heard the voice. The one you told me about. I heard it. And I saw your mother's room. The boxes half-packed. The clothes thrown about. You are unfinished. We are both unfinished. I want to go but not alone. I don't want to leave and wonder about you. That's all I've ever done is wonder about somebody else. I don't want you to be one of those questions. I couldn't help but come here. I saw the name of the town in the paper and I couldn't help it. I didn't think there was anything to be scared of. But I was wrong. He kept whispering to her through the remaining hours of the night. Sharing his time in the dark with someone else. Easing its burden.

Comfortable beneath its cover. She breathed heavy. Lost to this world, he thought. All the while she lay there listening to him and thinking, I will go if you ask me again in the light of day. I will go with you.

39

IT HAD ALMOST BEEN A game. Fuck up and see how quickly the news gets home. Fuck up and see if she'll be waiting on the porch swing when you get there. Fuck up and see if the bedroom door is locked. But on the day Dixon had shoved Colburn off the barstool there had been none of this. He followed routine, leaving the bar and driving around until late at night and then coming home. No lights on in the living room. Going inside and she wasn't sitting there. Going to the bedroom and the door was open and he waited for Sadie to say something but she didn't. He had stripped down to his boxer shorts, trying not to make a sound. Trying to slide into bed without waking her. Lying down and pulling the sheet across his chest and then she reached over and took the sheet and moved it from him. Slid her hands into his boxers and worked them down his legs and off his feet and she was naked and she crawled over him. Straddled him. Leaned and put her mouth to his and their bodies that had been so long strange to one another found familiarity in the dark. Aggressive with one another and wrestling with one another and working into a sweat through the deep and humid night. Each of them collapsing on their own side of the bed when it was done and they both slept in an unbothered sleep.

The next day when he left work he drove to the bar but

he did not stop. Instead he bought a twelve-pack at the gas station and then he went home and pulled two steaks from the freezer. He stopped the sink and ran warm water and then set the steaks down in the water to thaw. When Sadie came home an hour later she found him in the backyard sitting in the sunshine and sipping a beer and he told her to grab one and join him. She did. They kept on sipping while he lit the charcoal and grilled the steaks. Puffs of clouds passed across the sky in the evening breeze and the whir of a neighbor's lawnmower filled the silence. They had eaten outside, finishing the steaks just as twilight slipped away and then they were back in the bedroom and doing the same thing as the night before. The fitted sheet coming off the bed and a lamp knocked from the bedside table and the exhilaration of rediscovery.

And then the twins disappeared. Dixon showed up at the church parking lot every morning when the volunteers were divided into teams and he always raised his hand to go into the valley because he knew it was going to be the toughest search. He knew you would have to wrestle against the vines and step high and duck down and crawl around and whatever else but he wanted to be part of it. He wanted to be there when the twins were found. He wanted to walk in the house like a man and say we did it because that's what he was beginning to feel like again. He showed up every morning filled with hope. And he came home every night broken with disappointment. Another day gone and another night to pass and they hadn't found anything. And he had expected that the anxiety that covered the town would set him and Sadie right back into the old and tired version of themselves but she kept on. Grabbing him in the kitchen when he returned from the search and rubbing her hands along the scrapes and scratches on his hands and arms and then pulling his sweaty t-shirt over his head and shoving him into the bedroom and sometimes not making it to the bedroom but instead the sofa or the hallway or wherever they could find some leverage. Later when they were done they would talk about the day spent in the valley. Talk about the twins. Lying together in the bedroom. On top of the covers. Passing a glass of tea back and forth. Then falling asleep with their legs touching.

He thought about her while he was in the vines. He thought about her in the days when the searching paused, when he returned to his office and watched the hours tick away. He thought about her when he stopped in the bar to see Celia. He wondered if he was missing something.

Dixon was sitting in his recliner in the living room before work and browsed yesterday's newspaper with one leg crossed over the other. Sadie shuffled into the kitchen wearing slippers and a robe and she poured two cups of coffee. She then took the cups into the living room. Set his cup on the table next to the recliner and then she sat down on the end of the sofa. Thin curtains allowed the morning light in and her green eyes stared at the wobble in the surface of the coffee.

Dixon folded the newspaper and dropped it on the floor. He stretched his arms. Picked up the coffee cup. He smiled at her but she did not give it back. She wore a towel wrapped around her head and she set down her cup and removed the towel. Pushed at her wet hair with both hands, thick brown locks bunched together like whips. She crossed her legs and her robe opened and showed her thighs and he gave her legs a wolfish glance as he took his first sip. She watched him and she uncrossed her legs and left them open for an instant, his eyes up into the space between her thighs and he held still with the cup at his lips until she shifted on the sofa and draped the robe back across her legs.

'You know that I know,' she said.

He blew on the coffee. Leaned back in the recliner.

'You know I know,' she said again.

'Know what?'

'I've been waiting for you to just admit it.'

'I've been here with you, Sadie.'

'Before all this.'

'I didn't do nothing.'

'Before, Dixon.'

'Before what?'

He shook his head as if giving up on a puzzle. Sipped the coffee.

'Pam was there,' she said.

He looked out of the window. Sadie folded her arms. He had never been a talker and never would be. If she never asked him a question she wondered if he would utter any sound at all and in their coming apart in the last months and years she had tried this experiment during their morning coffee. Sitting there in silence, waiting for him to be the first to speak. The first to say good morning or I got to get to work or I have a headache or did you sleep good or something. But she waited and waited and he just sat there until she prompted him and then he would answer and maybe a fraction of a conversation would follow and then he would get up and set his cup in the sink on his way out the door.

If they hadn't spent most of the waning hours of their first year together sitting in a bar she would have figured out earlier that he wasn't going to talk unless he had a drink and moody light and a lit cigarette but she hadn't put it all together in time and here they were. Sixteen years later. Barely past twenty when they married and different people living together now and two cars and a house that needed a new roof and a lawnmower that only sometimes cranked. And memories neither one of them wanted to talk about.

When Pam called weeks ago and told her she had seen Dixon knock Colburn from the barstool, Sadie was happy that she had something to talk about. Something to say that mattered. A fight to pick. But then she had decided to go about it a different way and instead of sitting in the living room with a bent brow she instead took off her clothes and lay down in the bed. And now a month later she was ready to put an end to the part of his life that kept her guessing.

Believing she had brought him that far in their weeks of lovemaking and comradery.

'I want you to apologize,' she said.

He looked up at her.

'Today,' she said.' When you get off work. That man hasn't done anything to you.'

Dixon coughed. Fidgeted in the recliner. And then he said I don't know where he lives and even if I did there ain't no way in hell I'm going to apologize. He didn't get hurt.

'It's a miracle,' she said.

'What?'

'That you know what I'm talking about now.'

'I never said I didn't.'

'You're going to find him and apologize.'

'No I'm not.'

'Oh yes. You are. And you want to know why?'

'I don't need to know why cause I'm not doing it.'

'Yes you are.'

'I don't even know where he lives.'

'Yes you do. He's in that building with the big window for the whole world to see.'

'I still ain't doing it.'

She uncrossed her arms and lifted her feet from the coffee table and stood. She moved in front of him. Opened her robe and dropped it from her shoulders and she stood there in her bra and panties. He looked into her belly button and then she touched her fingers to his chin and lifted. His head fell back and his eyes met hers.

'Do you like what we've been doing?'

'Yeah.'

'Do you like the way it's been feeling around here? Like we're people again?'

He nodded.

'You don't have to love me,' she said. 'Or even if you do, you don't have to love me as much as you love her. I watched you staring at her at the bar until I couldn't take it no more and then when I couldn't take it no more I let you go down there by yourself, knowing the daydreams running around in your head. You won't make a fool out of me no more. You won't fight about her and you won't talk about her. With nobody.'

She moved her hand from his chin. Reached down and took his hands and she opened his palms. Ran them up her legs. Across her stomach. And then she moved them around to her ass and held them there and said because if you ever do that shit to me again it will be the last time your hands touch me here or anywhere. I'll find what I need somewhere else and then you'll get to be the fool. So when you go to leave work today, don't come home. You go find him. You know where he is. You apologize and then you forget about her. And then we can keep living.

40

THE BELL ABOVE THE DOOR jingled as Sadie unlocked the beauty salon and stepped inside. She locked the door behind her and then she crossed the black and white checkered tile and plopped down in one of the two cushioned salon chairs. She raised her foot and pushed against the counter and the chair spun around and left her facing the other side of the salon. The wall was covered in a mural of Main Street. Complete with a stray dog and mothers and children and a man leaning against a lamppost.

She crossed the floor and straightened the magazines on the small table in the waiting area. She then went into the hallway and opened a closet door and she took out the easel and the canvas and a bucket filled with paints and brushes. She carried it all into the middle of the salon floor where she set the easel next to the mural wall and she set the bucket on the floor. Then she closed the blinds on the front windows and made sure the sign said closed.

The mural had been done by a trio of art students the town had hired to give the buildings new life. A sunflower patch decorated the exterior brick wall of the dry cleaner's at the end of the block. A moon and stars stretched along the side of the bar. Above the awning of the café a flock of black-winged birds flew across cotton-ball clouds. She stood close while the students worked in the salon, noticing the way the brushes moved and how they created scale of figures and how they mixed color. It's not so different from what you do, one of them had told her. You create. You have imagination. Or else nobody would be brave enough to get their hair done here. By the time the mural was complete, she thought she had seen enough to try it herself. There were no art supplies in Red Bluff so she closed up shop one day and she drove to Memphis and bought an easel and a stack of canvases. Paints and brushes and art books. She began to try and then she quit when it didn't come easy.

She pinned a black canvas to the easel. Stared at it and saw herself sitting at the tavern down the street from the art supply store. A late afternoon. Two bags of supplies on the floor next to the legs of her barstool and the slow roll of a blues guitar in the speakers above the bar. An empty beer bottle in front of her and she waved for another and then the tavern door opened and two men strode across the wooden floor and then sat down to her left at the corner of the bar. The bartender gave her a fresh beer and then moved down to the men and before she reached for the beer she slipped off her wedding ring. It was an impulse and she gave a quick look in the mirror behind the bar. Her eyes questioning herself between the liquor bottles. But you haven't done anything yet, she answered and she slipped the ring into her pants pocket. She then unbuttoned an extra button on her shirt while the men and bartender chatted and as the bartender poured bourbon over ice she unbuttoned another. Peeked down and looked at the curve of her breasts and then as the bartender set the drinks before the men she arched her back and laid back her head, her eyes on the ceiling. Her arms fell to her side and she stretched and listened to the music and felt the dark of the tavern wrapping around her and when she brought her eyes forward again, the men and the bartender were all looking at her. Noticing the skin of her throat and chest and she twirled the beer bottle with her fingers and waited to see if one of them would come over to her because there was nothing waiting for her at home.

A knock on the turquoise door interrupted her.

A gray haired woman was pointing to her watch.

'Not now,' Sadie said.

The woman kept pointing and then said something Sadie couldn't make out through the glass. She walked back to the closet and grabbed a wadded sheet from the shelf and then she went to the front door, unlocked it, and told the woman I'm sick and you'll just have to reschedule and then she tucked the top of the sheet over the door and closed it. The paint-splattered sheet covered the door window and on the other side the woman griped for another minute before giving up.

She returned to the canvas but her mind was not in the tavern anymore. She was not in Memphis. She was here in this town where she felt the weight of grief and apprehension they all felt. No answers for the missing and the tall tales growing taller each day and an underlying suspicion of everyone and everything. She lifted a paintbrush from the bucket and with the dry bristles she traced the rise and fall of a hillside and she could see the vines crisscross and thicken and penetrate the valley and she wanted to reach into the canvas and snatch the answer from the thicket.

She didn't believe for a second that Dixon was going to find Colburn and apologize. He had already left her. We have left each other, she thought. I pulled us back for a minute but you saw how he reacted when you told him to apologize. If he would've just nodded. Something easy. He's never really been there anyway. Maybe I haven't either. It's hard to remember being so young. It's hard to remember anything before the baby. He's not going to apologize and he's got all day to figure out some bullshit excuse for why he won't.

41

I DO LOVE HER, DIXON thought. I don't know why she can't get it through her head. I married her and tried like godalmighty hell to have kids with her and I take her down to Florida once a year and what the hell else am I supposed to do.

He sat behind his desk and tapped the end of a pencil against its edge. Trying to decide if he was going to lie and say he apologized to Colburn or actually apologize to Colburn but either way she had won.

Maybe she just don't know what love is, he thought.

The one thing he was certain of was that he did not like the idea of never being able to lay his hands on Sadie again. The image of her body in front of him, holding his hands pressed against her ass, looking up at her over her breasts and into her serious eyes that promised no more of her flesh if he didn't stop acting like a lovesick dog. It was an image that had stayed in the front of his mind all day while he ignored the ringing phone and the paperwork.

I knew it was all too good to be true.

He threw the pencil against the wall and shoved away from the desk. He was up now, hands on hips and he paced around the desk and sucked in his breaths and on his third lap around the desk he noticed the office secretary watching him through the door window and he stepped over and let down the blind.

In the last two years Dixon had gone from driving the big machinery to selling the big machinery and he didn't like it at all. But Sadie had damn near erupted when he told her the boss wanted to bring him in off the worksites and give him a chance to make some real money selling these rigs instead of driving them. So he said yes when he wanted to say no. He wanted to say I like it better out there, climbing up in the seat of a dozer or working the controls of an excavator or riding in the high seat of a motor grader. I'm good at it and I like the way the men stand around and nod because they know it when they see somebody handling one of these things the right way. I like the sunshine and the cold don't bother me and neither does the heat and I like climbing down out of the seat and smoking a cigarette and admiring my own damn work. I don't give a shit about real money, he wanted to say. Just let me keep doing what I'm doing. But Sadie had jumped around the kitchen in little hops and then grabbed his arm and dragged him into the bedroom and rode him with shrieks and smiles and he had said yes. I'll do it and thanks for the opportunity. And the next day she took him shopping and nearly emptied their checking account buying shirts and ties and pants with pleats. Socks and a navy sport coat. A black belt and a brown belt and a new wallet because his old wallet was frayed at the edges and you can't let people see you with a ratty wallet. You'll have to shave every morning too she said and they bought new razors and shaving cream that smelled like flowers and a bottle of cologne that made his eyes water. When he walked into the sales office for the first time, the secretary did not recognize him with his parted hair and slick face though she had handed him his paycheck every other Friday for the last ten years. She asked if he needed some help before it occurred to her this was Dixon and he said you're damn right I do.

He sat back down in the desk chair. Unbuckled his belt and unbuttoned his pants. They were fitting tighter now. So was his shirt collar. He leaned back in the chair and rubbed his hands across his face and down his neck. Pressed at his throat. Then he opened the drawer and took out a pack of cigarettes and a box of matches. The phone rang and he reached for the cord and yanked it from the wall plug. He lit a cigarette and then there was a knock on the door.

'What?'

'Why aren't you answering your phone?'

'I didn't hear it ring.'

'Then put your ears on your head.'

'Where the hell else would they be?'

'Don't get smart.'

'What do you want?'

'I want you to answer the phone when I transfer a call to you because when you don't answer it comes back to me.'

'Sorry.'

'So answer it.'

'I can't.'

'Why not?'

'It's tore up.'

'What exactly are you doing in there besides smoking?'

'I'm getting ready to leave. Just take a message if somebody calls.'

'I don't guess I got no choice,' she said and then a huff. He smoked and looked at the clock. It was two thirty. He then

opened the desk drawer and reached in and pulled out the
coaster. *Happy birthday* was scribbled across the Budweiser
logo in Celia's handwriting. The coaster she had used for
the free beer she had given him on his thirtieth birthday.
Because this will be the greatest decade of your life, she had
told him. Bullshit, he thought. And he remembered them on
the tailgate so many years ago. Looking at the moon. High
school only days away from being done. And he found the
courage to say what he wanted to say to her. I love you and
I probably always will. I just need to let you know. A tremor
in his voice and a tremor in his hands. It had begun to hurt
worse to hold it in and with the night and the moon and radio
playing something slow, he had told her. She sat silent for a
minute and then she walked out into the field and then back
again. She stopped in front of him and said you know I love
you too. Just not like that. Maybe one day I will. A maturation
and tenderness in her voice and not what he wanted to hear
but what he expected. But she had accidentally given him
hope. Maybe one day I will.

He held the coaster and felt the thrill of that night so
long ago when he had been courageous and it was why he
couldn't help it. When the twins disappeared and there were
no answers and anxiety leapt from their eyes during church
or passing on street-corners, he couldn't help but make the
suggestion that only one thing changed in this town. You
know that? That welding guy who moved in on Main Street.
The one who used to live here a long time ago. The one
whose daddy went crazy. He showed up and right after look
what happened. I know they talked to him about it but that
don't mean nothing. You know he was the last to see them
alive. He admitted that much. Making these suggestions to

whoever would listen. Drinking coffee in the break room in the morning at work. Drinking beer at the bar. Standing in line at the post office. Talking over the fence with the neighbor. He suggested it and some of them listened. Because they all needed someone to blame.

He set the coaster in the drawer and closed it.

'Colburn,' he mumbled.

He dabbed out the cigarette in the ashtray on his desk. He stood and buttoned his pants and fastened his belt. His keys and wallet lay on the file cabinet next to the door and he grabbed them and opened his office door and walked out, ignoring the secretary who called out for him to go out and find a better mood somewhere before you come back tomorrow.

42

ON THE DRIVE OVER TO the bar Dixon had been trying to figure out the most efficient and effective way to get credit for an apology without sounding like a wuss. He had settled on four swift words. I didn't mean nothing. It was quick and vague and specific enough all at once. And he was repeating it to himself as he came in the door. I didn't mean nothing. He wanted to get it out and over with.

The boy was there and he looked up when Dixon walked in. Stopped chewing for an instant. Then he wiped his mouth with a napkin like Celia had convinced him to start doing. Dixon sat down and Celia came from the swinging door between the shelves of liquor bottles behind the bar. She set a glass of tea down in front of the boy and he started eating again. Colburn stood in the back next to the pool table, holding a cue. He and Dixon exchanged a look and then Colburn turned to take a shot.

'What are you doing?' Celia asked.

'Nothing.'

She spoke to him with her back turned. She wore a yellow sundress, shoestring-straps across her shoulders. Dixon admired her. Looking down at the back of her calf and to a rubbery scar that came from a day in the woods when they were kids. Celia sliding down an embankment and cutting the back of her leg on a jagged rock. He wanted to ask her if she remembered that day. If she remembered trying not to cry and holding his arm as she limped out of the woods. It was almost out of his mouth when she turned to him not with those childhood eyes but instead with impatience.

'You quit?' she said.

'Nope.'

'You get fired?'

'I wish.'

'It's early.'

'I know it.'

'Then what are you doing?' she asked again.

'Take it easy. I'm here to sit.'

'You'd better be.'

'Can I get a beer?'

She reached into the cooler. Lifted out a bottle and slid it to him.

The boy finished eating and then he drank down the tea. He wiped his mouth again and Celia pointed to the clean fork and knife next to the Styrofoam container. You're supposed to use those. I told you it wouldn't kill you. He cleared his throat. Reached down and picked up a garbage bag filled with aluminum cans and he said I thank you before lifting the bag over his shoulder and walking out the door. Celia picked up the napkins and container and dropped them in the garbage. She then picked up the silverware and said no need to wash this.

'Where'd he come from?' Dixon asked.

'I don't know. He won't say. Or he can't say is more like it. I don't even think he knows.'

'Was that his daddy laid out in the churchyard that time?'

'I didn't bring it up. You can't say too much to him or he'll eat so fast you'd think it was going down whole.'

'I wonder if they talked to him,' Dixon said.

'Who?'

'The police.'

'About what?'

'About the twins.'

Celia folded her arms. Leaned her hip against the cooler.

'What?' he said.

'Is that what you do now? Just make up shit about everybody you see?'

He shifted on the barstool. Looked at the jukebox.

'I'm sorry,' he said.

'You think I don't know what you been trying to get people to think about Colburn?'

'I said I was sorry.'

'No you didn't. I made you say it.'

'Look,' he said. 'I'm not here for this. I'm here for something else.'

'God knows what that might be,' she said.

'Maybe it'll make you feel better.'

Colburn had leaned the cue against the wall and begun to walk slowly toward them while they talked. Dixon saw him coming and he repeated it to himself. I didn't mean nothing. Just say it and shake his damn hand and be done. Colburn came to him and Dixon sucked down his pride and extended his hand to Colburn.

'I didn't −'

He never finished as Colburn shoved him hard in the chest and he flew backwards off the stool, arms and legs flailing in a brief moment of suspension before hitting the floor.

'How's it feel, asshole?' Colburn said.

'Colburn!' Celia yelled.

Dixon was to his feet quickly, hands into fists. He threw a wild right that Colburn easily sidestepped. Colburn shoved him hard again and Dixon lost his balance, tripping over his own feet and stumbling headfirst into the cigarette machine. Colburn was going for him again when Celia hopped the bar and cut him off. When Dixon raised up he was bleeding from a cut on his forehead where he'd caught the corner of the machine.

'Stop it! Both of you.' Dixon was red-faced and huffing. Colburn hard-faced and ready. She pushed against Colburn and his weight stayed forward and Dixon said let him go. Let the son of a bitch go.

'You heard him,' Colburn said.

'Stop it, Colburn. Right now,' she said and she pushed him harder.

'Fucking weirdo,' Dixon said. He touched the cut, a line of blood down the side of his face and sliding down his neck.

Colburn backed away.

Celia grabbed a towel from the bartop and held it to Dixon and he snatched it from her.

'This is what you want right here,' he said. 'This is exactly what you want.'

'Stop talking,' she said.

Dixon pressed the towel to his forehead. The blood had dripped onto his shirt collar and he could hear Sadie already. I told you to stop making me look like a fool, she would say. Tough shit, he would answer. And then he began to laugh. He pulled the towel from his eye and he kept on. A short and sarcastic laugh and he looked at Colburn.

'I bet you don't even know,' Dixon said.

'Sit down,' Celia said.

'Does he?' he asked her. 'Does he know?'

'Be quiet.'

'You don't,' he said to Colburn. 'I can tell.'

'Know what?'

'About your daddy. And her momma. About all the little meetings they used to have over there at her house. Same house I believe you've laid down in a couple of times.'

'Shut up, Dixon.'

'He was fucking her good,' Dixon said. 'So good it started messing with his head. Least that's how it's been told.'

'What the hell is wrong with you?' Celia yelled. He only laughed again. A little harder. The blood ran down his face and he wiped it with his fingers. Smearing it across his cheek and neck.

'That's not true, Colburn.'

'You fit perfect together,' Dixon said. 'Both crazy. Like your mommas and daddys.'

She turned and slapped him.

'This is what you came here for?' she said. 'This is what you wanted to do today when you woke up? Get the hell out of here and don't ever try to come back. Not ever.'

The smile then left his face. He looked over at Colburn. 'Say something,' Dixon said. She grabbed Dixon by the arm and he let himself be dragged to the door. She kicked it open and pushed him out and then she locked it as it closed. Dixon stood there on the other side of the glass. Looking back inside at her. But she had already turned to Colburn.

43

'HE CAME TO OUR HOUSE, Colburn. But not for that,' she said. 'None of that shit was going on. He came to her for a reading. She tried to help him.'

'Is this part of it?' he said.

'Part of what?'

'Part of the story you and everybody else around here keep making up.'

He picked up the beer Dixon had left behind and drank. Then he started walking along the bar and toward the pool table. She called to him but he kept walking. Through the storage room and out of the back door. Across the alley and to the street and he walked to the end of the block and turned on Main Street. He finished the beer as he walked and he busted the bottle on the sidewalk and then he came to his building. He opened the front door and stopped in the middle of the room where he had been trying to construct some sort of teepee with sheets of rusted tin, wrapping it with barbed wire to hold it together. He looked around and grabbed a crowbar from the floor and with one great swing and one great crash the sheet metal and barbed wire crumbled into a rusted mess.

He carried the crowbar with him out of the back of the building and the boy was there, filling the shopping cart from a pile of scrap machine and engine parts Colburn had gathered. Colburn grabbed the cart and turned it over. Shoved the boy and said I better never catch your ass back here again. Then he climbed in the flatbed truck. He drove fast through downtown and fast on the road that led to the valley and he slid in the gravel driveway at Celia's house. Turning in fast. Driving between the pecan trees and around to the backyard and he slammed on the brakes and the truck slid and came to a stop with its front wheels in the kudzu and he got out and screamed across the valley.

Celia was right behind him. Seeing him speed past the bar in the flatbed and she ran out and hopped in her car and followed him. She drove around to the backyard and got out and he was swinging the crowbar at some imaginary foe.

'This is why I didn't tell you. Because I was afraid of how you'd take it.'

'I told you everything.'

'Colburn.'

'Everything.' He walked over to the circle of bricks and the aluminum chairs and he slammed the chairbacks, two loud twangs. Then he kicked over the bricks and kicked at the burned black nubs and ash. And he was gone. Somebody else now. His eyes ablaze with hate and alarm and she circled around him. Not wanting to leave him but wanting to stay away. He moved toward her, stalking. Swinging the crowbar by his side. She hurried around to the other side of her car and kept the vehicle between them. And then he paused. Turned toward the valley as if his name had been called. Then he walked toward the shed. She came around the car and followed. Calling him and keeping her distance and he threw open the door. Stood there in the doorway.

'Go away,' he said.

'It's not your place to tell me to go away from.'

'Go away,' he said again.

She started to answer but then realized he wasn't talking to her. He raised the crowbar and stepped inside. She ran toward the house as crashes and clangs came from the shed as Colburn fought the ghost. She climbed in her car and sped along the driveway, throwing rocks as she turned into the road. Foot to the floor and pushing it back to town.

She went to town hall and the cruiser wasn't there. She went to the hardware store and the cruiser wasn't there. She then drove over to the café and she ran inside and asked if anybody knew where Myer was but no one could answer. Call him and tell him to get to my house and tell him to hurry. She hustled back out and to her car and headed back for the house, unsure of how long she had been gone. Fifteen minutes. Twenty. Long enough.

She found the front door was thrown open. Screens torn and ripped from the windows. Small terra cotta pots from the front steps busted against a pecan tree and lying in ruined fragments. She stepped onto the porch and went inside.

'Colburn,' she called.

She passed through the hallway. Listening. She looked into the reading room and the trunk was turned over and the paper scattered across the floor. Across the hall her mother's bedroom door was open. She called him again. No answer. She stepped inside the bedroom and the gramophone had been smashed on the floor. She backed out of the bedroom and passed through the house, going outside and into the backyard. Two pieces of the sheet metal walls had been torn away and exposed the inside of the shed. Splintered shelves. Broken glass of mason jars. A dented gas can lay by the door.

She found him standing at the edge of the valley. Facing the sun and his shadow stretched behind him and his hand wrapped in a towel. His figure stiff as if dipped in concrete. She imagined his hands grabbing and throwing and breaking and shattering and she believed it was all there was to see.

What she could not see was that while he raged, he had never stopped talking. He had argued with himself about who he was and what he was doing here and he had screamed at his mother and screamed at his father and screamed at the motherfucker whose dog had killed his brother. He had screamed at himself and yelled at the gramophone when he slammed it down on the floor just like his mother had once done and he had yelled at the walls and the ceilings and floors and his body and his mouth had moved in destructive and abusive coordination until he had run out of people and things to blame and then he had run out of the house and across the yard and begun to argue with the valley. To scream out toward the voices or the ghosts or whatever the hell they all said was out there. He had stepped out into the kudzu and ripped the leaves from their vines and held them in his bleeding hands and raised them about his head as he yelled and bawled and chastised and then he had collapsed into the vines and lay there. Helpless in their hold.

44

SHE WALKED UP BEHIND HIM. He unwrapped the towel from his hand and dropped it on the ground. Blood dripped from his knuckles.

'I like it better without answers,' he said.

He walked over and picked up the crowbar and tossed it onto the back of the flatbed. Then he moved to the truck door.

'What are you doing?'

'I'm loading up everything I can find around this valley and around this town and I'm leaving.'

'I can explain what Dixon said.'

'Then you should have before he said it.'

'Where are you going?'

'It doesn't really matter.'

'I guess not,' she said. 'You're going to be wherever you go.'

'I'll be there. All these stories and secrets won't.'

Myer then turned into the driveway. He drove across the yard and stopped next to the flatbed. He got out and looked around. The screens in the yard. The busted shed. The blood from Colburn's knuckles dripping from his fingertips.

'What's going on?'

'It's okay,' Celia answered.

'Don't look okay. You do all this?' he asked Colburn. Colburn opened the truck door.

'I said did you do all this?'

'Yep.'

'It's fine,' Celia answered.

'How about you? Are you fine? You didn't sound fine when you ran in the café. At least that's what they just told me.'

Colburn climbed into the truck and cranked it.

'You need to hold on,' Myer said. He stepped over to the truck and slapped the door.

Colburn revved the engine.

'Kill it and get out.'

He shifted into reverse and the front tires eased back out of the kudzu. Myer slapped the hood and pointed at him as he backed into the yard and then he pulled his pistol. Colburn hung his arm out of the open window. Shook his head at the sheriff.

'I bet that thing don't even work.'

'You kill it right now,' Myer said. 'Don't move that truck another inch.'

Colburn shifted into drive. Let his foot off the brake. The flatbed crept forward and Myer yelled for him again to stop right there but Colburn pressed the gas, a cough of black smoke from the tailpipe as he turned the corner of the house and headed for the road. Myer holstered his pistol and ran for the cruiser. Grabbing the radio and calling a deputy for help before chasing after the flatbed.

Celia stood there alone for a moment. Then she walked in the back door and into the kitchen. She took a garbage bag from underneath the sink and she went into her mother's bedroom and began to pick up the broken pieces of the gramophone.

But then she paused. Looked out of the window. A bright afternoon and a powder blue sky. Cherry-red wasps tapped against the glass. She stood and walked back outside. Thinking of the spring down below the kudzu. Thinking of her friends riding their bicycles out here. Her mother taking a mason jar from the pantry and giving them a dill pickle. She and her friends going outside and making funny faces from the sour taste and then tossing the half-eaten pickles into the woods before going in. Sometimes walking and sometimes crouched and sometimes crawling as the vine cover rose and fell between trees and brush as they crept down the hillside. Making it to the spring. The faint trickle like some lullaby and cupping their hands and drinking. Taking their shoes off and sticking their feet in the cold and clear water and how it felt so good.

She looked down at her bare feet. Thought about how good it would feel now to sit there with her legs stretched out and her feet in the spring. He told her he had found it. He had cut a path. She went to her closet and grabbed a pair of tennis shoes and she slipped them on. And then she walked outside and across the yard and past the shed, to where the vine-draped woods began. She saw the cuts where he had swung the machete and she followed the path of cut limbs and slashed briars and thorns. The path winding as he searched and she imagined the whacks of the machete. Imagined him curious. Imagined him wanting to give her something and this was it. This path into her childhood so different from his path back to his. She wound between trees and squatted beneath the low drapes, moving deeper down.

And then she saw the gathering of rocks, slick and shiny with the water spilling out from the earth. The spring still strong and lapping against the rocks and flowing down into the valley over flat stones and mounds of clay and hard red dirt. The same gentle song.

She knelt at the rocks. Dipped her fingers into the water and then touched them to her face. Then she sat down. She took off her shoes and touched her toes into the water. Cold and giving a chill up her calves and she smiled. Remembering its touch. And then she set her feet down into the spring.

45

COLBURN WASN'T RACING. HE DROVE casually back to town. Myer behind him, flashing his lights and waving his hand out of the window. Colburn waved back. He drove behind his building and parked in the alley.

Myer followed and was out of the cruiser and coming toward him before Colburn could kill the engine. From the other end of the alley, a deputy turned in and blocked the passage.

'Put your hands up,' Myer said.

'What for?'

'You know what for.'

'Can I get out first?'

Myer took a step back. Colburn opened the truck door and stepped out. He held up his hands and said let's get this over with so I can get the fuck out of here. Myer snatched his wrist and spun him around, cuffing one wrist and then the other.

The deputy joined them from the other end of the alley. Myer spun Colburn around and told the deputy to hold him.

'What the hell happened to your hands?' Myer said.

'We talked about this already,' Colburn said. 'When you sat me down and asked me about the twins.'

'Tell me again.'

'I work with metal. Steel. Heat. Tools. My hands get busted up sometimes.'

'That's fresh blood. I didn't see you working out there. Any of that blood belong to Celia?'

'God no.'

'It better not.'

'Look,' Colburn said. 'I lost my temper. I tore up some stuff out there but she wasn't there. I'll go back and fix it all.'

'Yeah,' Myer said. 'You will.'

'Fine.'

'Right now.'

'I heard you.'

'Let him go,' Myer told the deputy. The deputy turned loose of Colburn's arm.

'You want me to uncuff him?' the deputy asked.

'No,' Myer said. 'He can wear them a minute or two longer. Until he's good and relaxed. You can go.'

Colburn leaned his back against the truck and watched the deputy walk the alley and climb back into his cruiser.

'What's going on, Colburn?' Myer asked. The muscles in Colburn's jaw tightened. He shook his head.

'Celia runs in the café, says to get word to me that I need to get out to her house. Then I show up and you're bleeding and she's got the look of worry all over her face.'

'I don't have nothing to say to you. I don't have nothing to say to anybody. All I want to do is get my hands free and load my truck and drive out of here. That should make everybody happy.'

'How about you? That make you happy?'

'That's what I said.'

'You're not going anywhere until you go back out to the house and fix it back like you found it.'

'I know.'

'Then turn around.'

Colburn turned to the side and Myer unlocked the cuffs. 'Do I need to follow you back out there?' Myer asked. Colburn rubbed at his wrists. He pulled his shirt over his head and used it to wipe the blood from his hands and fingers. Then he tossed it into the open window of the truck and said follow me if you want. Follow me if it'll keep you busy. Last I heard there were two children you can't seem to find and I bet their momma would be real happy to know you got shit else to do besides tail me around.

46

He's right, Myer thought. I don't know what to do. I
don't know what in the hell I'm supposed to do. He
sat in the cruiser parked next to the mailbox. He looked at
the spot on the ground where Colburn had seen the roll of
barbed wire and fence posts. He looked at the magnolia tree
next to the house where Colburn said the twins were playing.
He remembered the crowd of men going in and out of the
house in the days after, asking questions the mother could
not answer. Looking for evidence that wasn't there.

He got out of the cruiser and sat on the hood. Looked
at the valley that surrounded the house and yard. Watching
for something he should have seen before. Some answer that
might raise its head from a tangle of vines and say I'm over
here. What you are looking for is right over here. Get off your
ass and come get me. He opened the mailbox, the mail piled
up as the mother had gone to stay with a cousin in town. He
closed it again and he crossed the yard and stopped at the
magnolia tree. Turned around and looked up and down the
road and tried to believe the conclusion they had come to.
The twins were outside when a vehicle stopped. For whatever
reason, by force or seduction, the twins got in the vehicle and
then they were gone. It was simple and logical because there
was no trace. But the simple and logical did not sit well with

Myer and it did not sit well with the people he had to face every day.

I should have something better to do but I don't know what that is, he thought. How are you supposed to know? One minute you're dragging a deer off the side of the road and the next minute the whole town is looking at you for answers and you don't have any. He shook his head. Looked down at the ground at his own shadow. Knowing his entire life he had been walking toward this point of great expectation and wishing he would have paid better attention. Sharpened those things inside him that needed to be sharpened. These things happen to people and you are not ready. You are becoming an old man who is giving nothing. An old man with a limp.

He walked back to the cruiser. Go back to the office and read everything again. Read it like it's the first time. Read what Colburn said about that afternoon. Maybe there's a word there that means more. Maybe. He took one more look around. The hillsides covered in green. The ups and downs of the suffocated. He cranked the cruiser and pulled into the road and the engine heaved as he pushed the gas pedal, drowning out the cry that came from somewhere below. Unaware of how close he had been to becoming the hero he wished he could be.

47

THE BOY STOOD AT THE edge of the valley. He left the shopping cart in the roadside weeds and he was about to go under when he heard the scream from beneath. A shrill cry muffled by the vines. He looked up and down the road. Thought maybe it was some animal he had never heard before. Then there was another scream and he knew it was a woman. Maybe their woman come back from wherever she had been and her and the man picking up where they left off. There was one more shriek and it was not the scream of argument or hate but it was the sound of bad dreams and he knew the difference. He looked in the direction that the screams had come from and he watched for movement, little humps of struggle from beneath. But the valley lay still. He waited for another scream but there was only silence.

48

WHEN MYER LEFT HIM, COLBURN went inside and put on a clean t-shirt. Then he ran his hands under the faucet, rinsing away the blood. He took a sock and tied it around his knuckles. Drank from a nearly empty bottle of bourbon. Then he grabbed his toolbox and returned to the flatbed.

He didn't know what he was going to say when he returned to Celia's house. I'm sorry. That would be a good start, he thought. Goodbye. That's what he promised he was doing, loading up and leaving but he didn't want to say that. He parked in the gravel and got out and walked around to the back of the house. He set the toolbox down. Picked up the aluminum chairs and pushed at the crowbar dents, trying to flatten their backs but they were forever disfigured. He rearranged the circle of bricks. He kept waiting for her to come from inside the house or from the shed. He kept waiting to hear his name or maybe he had done it. Maybe she wouldn't say it anymore.

He walked around the house, picking up the screens he had torn away. Picking up the gutter drain he had kicked free. Picking up the broken terra cotta pots and setting it all in a pile of debris that he would later have to calculate for a list at the hardware store.

Maybe I should be the one to go to her, he thought.

He went inside the house. Moving from room to room and calling her. There was no answer and no movement so he walked into the backyard. Silence all around. He checked her car and the keys were in the ignition. Her cigarettes on the dashboard.

He walked down the slope of the backyard and stopped at the kudzu. He called out her name, his voice falling down into the valley like a feather from the sky. Weightless and insignificant. He called three and four and five times, each time his voice growing louder and beginning to rise with the tone of uncertainty. Not calling her emphatically as before. Celia. But calling out a question. Celia? Celia?

He went to the shed and found the machete. The blade stuck down into the ground. He then faced the sun once more as it settled low over the hillsides and burned across the rich green leaves. He screamed out her name. Clutching the machete and screaming and knowing she would not answer and instead hearing the voice saying come on. Come on down here.

He only knew one way in and that was the path he had cut. The direction of the spring. He stomped into the woods and followed his own trail. Calling her. Swinging the machete. Ducking the smothered branches and limbs and pushing away the vines. Twisting and turning down the slope and tripping once and rolling. Dropping the machete but then rising in a hurry and snatching it by the handle and keeping on and then he saw the gray black rocks and the moss growing on their sides. He saw the clear water rising from the spaces in between and flowing down through this world below. And he saw her shoes next to the spring and he saw the spot where she had been sitting but she was no longer there.

49

COLBURN STAYED UNDER. SLASHING AT the undergrowth and the vines that smothered them. Going further down, moving through gullies and stepping over fallen trees. Calling Celia as he sweated in search and panic. Talking to himself in between. Trying to find reasons for her shoes to be there and for her to be somewhere else. She doesn't like to wear them anyway. She walked out of the valley on some other side and hitched a ride back to town and now she's sitting at the bar. Legs crossed like she always does. Flipping the Zippo like she always does. She's tired of talking to you and she's hiding from you. That's all.

The light began to fade.

He chopped and sliced and when his foot got caught in a twist of vines he swung down as if there were hands reaching up from the grave and he sliced his boot. A moment later he felt the warmth of the blood. He dropped the machete and pulled his boot off. There was blood and there would be more. The vines were just above his head and he reached up and pulled them apart. The sun was dipping closer to the horizon and he gripped the machete. Pulled his boot back on and raised his shirt and wiped his face and neck. Panting and sweating and all around him this smothered land. The throbbing of his foot and the blood in his sock and the blood on his hands and his chest heaving while the question burned through his skull. Where is she?

He looked back up the hillside at the stretch of pathway he had cleared, the crooked and butchered trail. He called her name again. The daylight fading and the shadows coming and as he stepped over and around rotted limbs and animal carcasses and snake skins he felt the consciousness of this otherworld as if what was hidden below was not dead but very alive. The air stagnant but seeming to pulse in a hot and heavy breath and not the dull silence that he expected but instead something of a hum. A low and singular note sung by the earth itself. He hacked and crept and crawled and then he would stop when he could stand again. Look around. His sense of direction slipping away and shadows moving in a shadowless world and the deep and hypnotic hum. He came to a space between a gathering of pines and he dropped the machete. A burning blister now inside his thumb and bristles in his hair and on his clothes and he leaned against a tree.

Then he dropped down to his knees. Clawed at the earth as if digging for some answer that may have been buried in that exact spot. Not knowing why but digging until his hands were covered in clumps of bloodied dirt. And then he collapsed. Rolled onto his back. Through the vines he saw the lavender sky.

She's at the bar. Get up and get out of here.

He came up from the valley and through the woods like some murderous caricature. Wielding a machete. Blood on his shirt and jeans. Blood in his boot. A grimy face and neck. Emerging out of a nightmare and into reality. He hobbled past the shed and across the yard. He sat down in an aluminum chair and he dropped the machete on the ground.

The hillsides lathered in the dying light. Something howled. He stared out into the coming night and tried to imagine her laughing.

50

THE BOY HID INSIDE THE vinecovered house until dark. Wanting to go and look but waiting for the cover of night and when it came he began to move about the valley. He carried a cigarette lighter that he used to light his steps. The singular flame on and off again. Not wanting to be seen. He would move some and then he would sit and listen. The rustles of the nocturnal moving around him. Small things that kept his head turning from side to side and kept him alert as he was looking for the big thing on two legs. The humped shadow at odds with itself.

He moved beneath ridges. Rose out of the kudzu onto a bluff. Sank back down and crept along a ditch. He sat down on the ground with his back leaned against a fallen tree. His head leaned back and his eyelids heavy and he was almost asleep when he heard the man talking to himself.

He sat up straight. The voice sounding like it came from all sides and he could not settle on its direction. A steady stream of deranged conversation off in the dark interrupted only by the smack smack smacking of his tongue and gums. The boy moved quietly to his knees. Quietly to his feet. Leaned his head forward as if that might somehow improve his night vision. The voice was moving and then he heard the man stumble and fall. A quick shout of curses that came from directly out in front of the boy. He moved forward a single step and the man seemed to lie still. The boy moved forward again but then stopped when he heard the man move and start talking again and now he could make out his black figure.

The man kept talking. A series of questions and answers that circled around and around and sometimes his voice rose in defiance against his own question and other times he mumbled like a penitent child. He talked and he moved and the boy followed until the man came to a ridge. There he paused. A quick flick and the tiny dot of matchlight. The man making sure of his steps. The man then blew out the match and the boy watched him climb the ridge. Standing on top he struck another match. Gave himself some final command. And then he disappeared down into the cave.

51

COLBURN SAT FACING THE VALLEY all night. Dozing in and out of sleep. When the sun began to rise, he stood from the chair. His aching forearm from swinging the machete. His rough and damaged hands. With the first step he felt his wounded foot and he grimaced. Sat back down. He took off his boot. His sock a crust of dried blood that he peeled from his skin.

He limped inside the house and went into the bathroom. He took off his clothes and turned on the shower and stepped in. The dirt and dried blood flaking away. The wounds on his hands and foot beginning to bleed again. He got out of the shower and sat on the toilet seat, pressing a towel against the slice on his foot to slow the bleeding. Thinking of what to do.

He dressed in the filthy shirt and jeans and carried his boots and bloodied sock with him as he went outside to the truck. He drove into town. The diesel engine chugging and breaking the silence of the early morning. He parked behind his building and went inside and put on clean jeans and a shirt. He had a roll of gauze and he cut strips of fabric from an old shirt and he wound a strip around his knuckles and wrapped it in gauze and then did the same to his foot. He pulled on clean socks and then he tried to wash the blood from his boot over the sink. He then slipped it on and layered several strips of duct tape across the cut of the worn leather. His dirty clothes lay in a wad and he scooped them up and walked out and tossed them into the dumpster in the alley.

He drove over to the bar and pulled on the door. He knew if she was around, she would be here at lunch for the boy and that was what he believed he was waiting for. And I won't tell her of all the horrible shit I'm imagining. I'll just tell her I'm glad to see her. I'm not going anywhere. I'm a sorry son of a bitch and I'll never let you see that side of me again. I don't care what you did or didn't tell me about my father coming to see your mother. I don't care. That's all gone. He tugged on the door once more as if he was on the other end of a bad joke and then he returned to his building. He sat on the floor and stared out of the window at the people passing along the sidewalk. At the slow-moving shadows as the morning sun crept higher. He was tired and shadow-eyed and then his head leaned forward and he fell into a half-sleep and dreamed of Celia's house and her mother come back, a frazzled woman standing in her bedroom and looking for the photographs on the wall that had been taken down and put into a box, looking for the faces of her past and wondering where they must be and she carried a long knife, a white-knuckle grasp around its handle and her thin legs and her old and shriveled body, the skin gray and hanging and the voices of the valley now a part of her as she moved along the hallway without sound and without weight like some ghoul that simply inhabits the cross and evil air that surrounds. Coming to the door of the bedroom where Colburn and Celia slept and wondering who was lying next to her daughter and he woke with a jerk. Panting and big-eyed. Filled with the certainty that someone or something was in the building with him and he waited for a footfall or threatening voice. But there was only the pale light of noon.

He drove back to the bar but she wasn't there. He expected to find the boy waiting but he wasn't there either. He drove out to her house and nothing had moved and he stood at the edge of the kudzu and waited for her to come up from the trail and say I thought I'd never find my way out of there. Didn't mean to worry you. Let's go to the bar and get a beer. He then looked across the valley and remembered what she had told him about the house buried down below. Remembered what she had said about her mother believing there are things out there that connect us. Save us. He spotted the mound of vines covering the house in the belly of the valley. The chimney wrapped in green and reaching toward the sky in a hopeless plea for mercy. He grabbed the machete and went back under.

52

THE BOY WAITED ALL NIGHT for the man to come out of the hole he had disappeared down into. He then waited as the dull light of day bled down through the vines. He waited as the birds began to sing. He waited as the morning dragged on and the temperature rose and the air grew more stagnant beneath. Then he moved over to the ridge and crawled up and he stood at the edge of the cave. Looking down. Seeing the bottom. Growing brave.

He dropped down into the opening. On the ground were nubs of candles and he picked up the one with the most length and he lit it with the lighter. He began an unhurried descent into the tunnel and in the candlelight he saw things. Food wrappers. Random pieces of clothing. Chicken bones. Empty beer cans. A steady trail of litter as he moved along and then the smell grabbed him. Beyond foul. The smell came to him on the wind that moved through the tunnel and it caused him to bend over and cough. He moved a little further in and he dry-heaved. His muscles tight and his eyes watering as he gagged and gagged. When he raised up again he lifted his shirt over his nose and mouth and pinched his nose and the air became more rank and deathlike with each step further into the tunnel. But he walked on deeper into the dark with nothing but his own shadow and fear. The flame wobbling and the rancid air and he wished he had something to swing. A hatchet or a stick or anything besides a candle which would be no good against the monster he believed he was going to find. Every few steps he stopped. Paused. Listened for the man talking to himself but there was only the moan.

The boy stopped at the edge of the pit and held the candle toward the great pool of nothingness. The earth having fallen away from all sides and the pit now reached from one side of the tunnel to the other. A black abyss below and no way around it. And the smell that had kept him coughing and gagging was rising from the pit as if it had been released from the guts of hell.

The boy reached down and dug his finger into the earth and then set the candle in the space he created. He called out some indistinguishable word and did not expect an answer but then he heard the movement from the far side of the pit, from deeper in where there was no light. A moaning reply and the dragging of lazy steps through the rock and dirt and then he appeared in the soft light of the candle. He was naked and covered in the black earth and his eyes bulged from his taut and drawn face. It was the man but it was not the man. Here was the prisoner in his own gruesome world.

The boy stepped back. He looked at the man. At his dirt-covered face and head. At the open and dry mouth. Claw marks across his chest and neck. Bony fingers dangling from bony hands.

The man had set Celia's body next to the pit. Removing the yellow dress. Lying there beside her and resting with his head on her stomach. Telling her things in the same way he had done to the twins. Incoherent promises of lives better lived here in the dark with him. Lifting her fingers and touching them to his own face. Buried in the black. Solace against her body while vengeful against her world. And then when he was finally ready to send her down into the pit with the woman and the twins, he lit a candle and took a final long and tormented look at her naked body and then he lifted her legs and dragged her closer and the earth crumbled, the sides falling from the pit and he had no choice but to jump and he caught hold on the other side and clawed and crawled as the dirt and rock fell away in chunks and it did not stop until gravity had cleared the pit from one side of the tunnel to the other. The space left behind too far to reach across and likely impossible to leap.

The candle had disappeared with the pieces of earth. And then there was the dark and only the dark and the moan from deep below. The man had stripped himself naked and rolled in the dirt and felt the jagged rocks bruising and cutting and he no longer smacked because there was no more saliva and now he stood at the edge of the pit and stared across at the boy. His mind distrustful of what he saw as he had dreamed of rescue. He raised his arm and held his hand out to the boy.

'Help me, son,' he said.

The boy picked up the candle and he moved it around the tunnel. Looking for a length of vine or root. Anything that he might be able to extend to the man. The putrid smell in his nose and mouth and he gagged as he moved along the tunnel and then he saw Celia's dress. Wadded and on the ground next to the cracked glass of the oil lamp. The boy picked it up by the thin shoulder straps and he shook the dirt from it. The yellow of the candlelight and the yellow of the dress glowing together and giving him the answer he both wanted and did not want. He then draped the dress over his arm and he moved through the tunnel, returning to the pit where the man was on his knees now. An expanse of black between them. His hands resting on his thighs in a posture of repose. As if having come to some prayerful resolution.

The boy pointed at the man. Then he pointed down into the pit. And then as the boy turned around and began to leave the tunnel, he heard the shuffle of earth and the feeble cry of falling.

53

H E WORKED TO MAKE IT down into the belly. Cutting and crawling. Losing direction and then finding it again.

Pulling vines and pushing limbs and then he was finally there. Colburn stared at the house and felt as if he had been transported into another realm. That he was caught in some black-and-white photograph that gave no inclination as to time or place.

Do you have any answers for me? he thought.

He moved across the porch. Leaned the machete against the doorframe and he walked into the hallway. He touched his fingers to the rough plaster walls and he was nearly to the end of the hallway when he felt the deep cut into the plaster. He stopped and stepped back and carved into the wall was a stick figure. On the floor beneath the stick figure was a scattered pile of chalky crumbles. The figure stood almost as tall as him. An egg-shaped face. No eyes and no mouth. He moved his finger along each arm. Down the trunk. Along both legs.

Colburn looked down the hallway and to the open door. Making sure the machete was still there. And then he asked the house again. Do you have any answers for me? All I need is one answer. One something. You have been here for so long. You know what's down here. Help me.

A storm was moving into the valley now and the rain had begun to fall and the wind sang down through the vines and he listened for what the house could say to him. So many had claimed that this valley spoke to them and maybe it has spoken to me too but I don't need a maybe right now. I need an answer and I need to know if she is here somewhere. He kept asking his questions and hoping for answers and then the voices of the valley came in a chorus of wind and rain and he raised his hands and pressed them flat against the stick figure. Dropped his head and closed his eyes and the house spoke.

I'm like you, it said. I've been so lonely. Buried by time. So far away. There once were voices here. There once was laughter. I gave them fire in the winter and the smoke rose from my chimney and reached into the night, rising toward the stars and proving that I belonged. In the spring the footsteps of children knocked against my floors and wild roses grew next to me and gave rich pink blooms and when it rained they stood on the porch and held their hands under the runoff from the roof and splashed the water on one another and behaved like children are supposed to. Sometimes the children cried and sometimes the mother and father cried but it never lasted long and I held them and they held one another but one day they left and they did not come back. I waited and waited and I watched the years go by and I felt the rain and I felt the heat and the birds nested inside and the wolf dragged its prey onto my porch and I believed they would return. But no one returned and then as the years went on I began to watch the vines creeping across the hillside. Moving across the valley without discrimination and taking the land and taking the trees and the blooms and I knew it was coming for me. It moved so slowly but I never stopped watching and all I needed was one of them to return and see what was happening to the valley and to see what was going to happen to me. All I needed was one of them to come back and take out their blade and cut it back. I was going to disappear and I never took my eyes from the vines as they slithered right up next to me. Slid under me. And then began to crawl up my sides and through my floorboards and over my roof and no one came. Now I'm gone and I belong to the kudzu just like everything else here belongs to it and I knew there was evil in its growth and in its reach. How can you stop such evil?

Tell me, Colburn thought. Tell me all of it.

No matter how long it has been since I have felt the laughter and the pulse of life I know that what moves in and out of me now does not belong and in those nights when I'm afraid I pray for the earth to open up beneath me and swallow us all so that no one else has to feel what I feel inside and I want to close my doors and windows and hold it hostage like the vines that hold me hostage but my windows are broken and my doors are crippled. So there is only fear. They left me here.

And no one told me it would be this way. I thought that being alive meant something else. Why did they make me? Only to leave me this way?

I don't know, Colburn answered. I don't have any answers for you. But do you have any answers for me. That is what you can do to feel alive again. You can give me an answer because I am like you and I wonder the same things. Why did they make me to leave me this way? But you are not as alone as you think because she talked about you. Can you feel that? Celia pointed out here and said you existed. Not everyone forgot you. And there are others who remember you. I bet those children remember you and remember the rain from your roof and the fires in your chimney. They remember their mother in your kitchen and their father putting them to bed. Those are things that cannot be taken away and those children and their mother and father are out there and remember you. You are inside of them like they were once inside of you and you are in their dreams. Does that make you feel alive?

I'm afraid. That's how I know I am alive.

Colburn opened his eyes. Removed his hands from the wall. He stood still in the hallway and listened to the storm and then he repeated what the house had said to him. I'm afraid. That's how I know I am alive. And he knew that if he moved from this spot he would see him. He knew that if he walked to the end of the hall and looked inside one of the rooms, any of the rooms, he would see his father swinging from the ceiling beam and his eyes would be open and pleading and resentful and broken all at once. The eyes he could never read and the eyes he always searched for tenderness and he knew his father was here and swinging and waiting to set his eyes on Colburn again. He stood still in the dull gray. In the black-and-white photograph that was fading and weathered and he did not want to see him and then he heard his mother call from another room. Her voice faint and trembling like a trickle and he pressed his hands over his ears and squeezed his eyes closed and refused to listen to them or see them but he knew they were there. His mother calling and his father swaying and he doubled over and rocked and grunted and then the thunder rumbled and it came as the sound of the dog, the low growl as it stood with its head poked between the space in the fence, the low growl as it watched and waited and then changed them all, the living and those yet to be born. And the house said I told you so. I told you. There are things here that shouldn't be here and now you feel it too. And then Colburn raised up and screamed back at the house. Shut up. Either help me or shut the hell up. I'm not looking for them because I'm looking for Celia and either goddamn help me or shut up.

I told you, it said again.

He was breathing hard now. Gasps of despair. He opened his palms and looked at the blisters and cuts and he tried to slow himself. To remember why he was down here. He then moved to the end of the hallway and looked into each of the back rooms. One was the kitchen. In the other room was a fireplace and a mound of leaves large enough for a man and the depression was covered with a blanket. Colburn reached down and pinched the corner of the blanket with his thumb and index finger and he lifted it from the nest. Once upon a time it had been sky-blue but now it was faded and gave a putrid smell. He stretched out his arm and wrinkled his nose and as he dropped it back onto the nest he noticed that he was surrounded by more stick figures. The walls covered with them. Some of them tall and some of them like children. Some of them holding hands. And on the floor beneath the crowd of stick figures he recognized his own chisel and long-handle flathead screwdriver, surrounded by the crumbles of plaster like dirty fallen snow. In the far corner of the room was a pile of things that had belonged to Celia.

Colburn knelt at the odd gathering of souvenirs. Cocktail napkins from the bar covered in notes she had scribbled, a cigarette lighter, a pair of sunglasses. He thought he heard a footstep and he stood. Looked toward the doorway. And then he saw her dress, hanging from a nail on the wall. He stepped through the bed of leaves and snatched it from the nail. Held it up by the straps and it was filthy and torn but it belonged to her. There was no doubt and then he knew it was the boy and he saw it all. He saw the boy waiting outside the bar and following them out to the valley. He saw the boy hiding in the valley beneath the vines and watching Celia as she came down the pathway. He saw the boy using Colburn's own stolen tools as weapons to do whatever he had done to her. He spun and looked around the room once more before tucking the dress under his arm and he had taken one step into the hallway when he heard the footstep and saw the shadow just as the back of the shovel blade clanged against his forehead and all went dark.

54

IXON DROVE ALONG THE BACKROADS. The storm having blown through and a light rain trailing behind. The cool air that follows. The sense of something changing.

The road was narrow and rutted. Rainwater filling the potholes. Thick tree limbs reaching over the fence line. He had walked out of his office and rolled up his sleeves. Pulled off his tie and unbuttoned his shirt collar. Stopped at the gas station and bought a twelve-pack and cigarettes and then he had stopped by the salon and asked Sadie if she wanted to ride with him. Let's just go riding and drinking and listening to music. Like we used to do. But then she asked if he had apologized to Colburn like he was supposed to do and he pressed his teeth together and frowned. It's raining, she had answered.

He drove alone. The window down and the rain on his arm and touching the side of his face and it felt good. Felt damn good. He kept the radio low and the truck tires bumped through puddles. The countryside soggy and slick looking. He thought of the stretch of rainy days when the twins had disappeared. The grasp of the vines. The howl of the dogs. The slippery rises and falls. Dixon right there with them, the searchers frustrated by their inability to move more quickly and cover more ground. He remembered the hurt he felt, the hurt they all endured when they found nothing and kept on for days and weeks finding nothing and how weak it felt to tell the mother they found nothing and promising they would keep looking and still finding nothing.

He had imagined it being his own son disappearing. Their child born when it was supposed to be born and growing strong and one night after they searched until dark he had slipped into the church sanctuary. The great room calm and drenched in shadow. The solitude and tranquility comforting him as he stood at the altar and raised his eyes to the stained glass window that was high on the wall above the pulpit. The outstretched arms of Christ. The crown of thorns. The crimson wrap around his waist. Dixon stood there in the dark. Whispering a prayer for the twins and for the miracle of finding them and then the prayer had shifted into a plea for his own life slipping away. Not able to name or understand the emptiness but asking that it go away. Let it go away. When he was done he lowered his eyes from the stained glass and paced the aisle, the heels of his boots knocking against the hardwood floor and making echoes in the quiet place with the high and arching ceiling and he imagined someone there with him. Someone listening.

He finished a beer and tossed the can into the floorboard.

A few of them there now. He opened another and turned on his headlights as the land was draped in gray, the cloud cover bringing an early night. He came to a four-way stop and turned right and in another half-mile he stopped at a mailbox. He opened it and pulled out two envelopes and then he shut the box. Turned into the driveway and followed the messy road, his tires sliding some and splashing more and then he came to the trailer. He turned his headlights on the front door and blew the horn. A head poked out and Dixon yelled out of the truck window. Come on and let's ride.

The door shut. Random tires lay around the yard. A dog with her teats dragging came around the side of the trailer and regarded the truck before slipping beneath the makeshift porch. Morning glory grew out of a cast-iron tub. The door opened again and a woman came out. She wore a jacket with a hood pulled over her head and cut-off jeans that fit ten years ago. She crossed the mushy yard on her tiptoes and when she got in the truck she said I guess you think you can just pull up to a woman's house and blow the horn and she'll come running.

'Well,' he said. 'You did.'

She removed the hood from her head and pushed her hair around with her hands. She then took a beer from the twelve-pack carton and unzipped the jacket.

'Here's your mail,' he said and he passed her the envelopes. She took them and set them on the dashboard.

'I don't figure that's what you came here for. To deliver my mail.'

'Nope.'

'You said something about riding?'

'I did.'

'Then ride.'

Dixon turned around in the yard. He lit a cigarette and she took one from him. He drove carefully along the sloppy driveway back to the road. The rain had stopped and the sky stretched out in blends of gray and purple. She turned up the radio and tapped her fingers on top of her knee. They sipped their beers and eased on through the wet country. She looked over her shoulder at the shotgun on the rack in the back window and said when's the last time you shot that thing.

'Long time,' he said. 'I don't ever hardly go in the woods no more.'

'You still can.'

'I suppose,' he said. 'You know where I spend my time. Same place as you. Why aren't you at the bar anyway?'

'Why aren't you? You been shamed out?'

'I wish that was all there was to it.'

'It's not open anyhow,' she said. 'I heard Myer had to go out to her house because of that old boy.'

'Who? Colburn?'

'Yeah.'

'What for?'

'I don't know. I rode by there coming home from work today and there was a bunch of shit tore up in the yard.'

'Like how?'

'Nevermind. Damn it. I shouldn't have said nothing.'

'Let's go see.'

'I don't want to.'

'How come?'

'Cause soon as we go in that direction this ride'll be over and we haven't even got started good.'

'Just show me.'

'You gotta stop.'

'I know it. That's what I keep hearing.'

'I mean it, Dixon. You're gonna come home and Sadie will have your shit all boxed up if you don't quit it. This guy has got you all worked up. For nothing.'

'It ain't for nothing.'

'Then what's it for?'

He sucked on his cigarette. Drank his beer. The truck wandered in the middle of the road.

'Let's ride then,' he said.

'She might even box you up for riding around out here with me.'

'I asked her first.'

'So I'm second choice or third.'

'You're not any choice. Drink and smoke and ride. Is that so damn hard?'

'Fine,' she said. She opened another beer and took another cigarette from his pack on the bench seat.

'You know what,' he said. 'We'd better go see.'

'Come on, Dixon.'

'It won't take but a second if you'll promise to shut up,' he said.

'I'll promise to shut up if you promise you won't take me back and drop me off right after you see it.'

'I promise,' he said. They both knew he was lying. She moaned and crossed her legs. Shook her head. A fork in the road lay ahead and he veered to the right, moving in the direction of the valley. Then he hit the brakes. Came to a stop in the middle of the road. He shifted into reverse and then drive and then reverse and then drive, getting turned around. Telling her we'll have to do this some other time. Ain't no sense in pretending I'm not taking you back. She shifted in the seat and pouted and she did not talk anymore. She only smoked in little puffs of aggravation until they were back in her driveway.

55

WHEN COLBURN OPENED HIS EYES again it was night. He lay flat on his back on the floor and he tried to sit up but when he lifted his head he felt the rush of pain and then he touched his fingers to the bruise that stretched across his forehead. A vine reached through the gap in the floor and tickled his ear and he slapped it away and he sat up. Looked around. The rain had come and gone while he lay unconscious. Water dripped from the ceiling. Frogs groaned into the night. He wondered if he was alone. Wondered why it hadn't been worse.

He got to his feet and staggered a couple of steps and caught himself against the wall. Took Celia's dress from the nail. He wrapped it into a ball and walked out of the house and into the dark. Unsure of which way to go but he started anyway. Rainwater dripping from the cover above and he slipped and slid on the wet ground. He heard things moving in the dark and it kept his eyes darting back and forth and his pulse jumping, disoriented and dizzy and seeing creatures that may or may not have been there. Maybe she's here somewhere, he thought. Maybe there is another house or shed underneath that only the boy knows about and that's where he took her. Colburn ambled about in the wet dark. Trying to get out. Flashes of thought that made sense. The way the boy sat at the end of the bar when Celia fed him or gave him a cold bottle of Coke and he never said a word, only watched her with his head hung low, stalking her with his sunken and dark-rimmed eyes. Pushing the cart along the sidewalk in front of the bar more often. Coming inside more often. Sitting in the same spot and nodding and staring and he didn't know where the boy could have hidden or how he could have known she was down by the spring but it did not matter how it all fit together, the dress was the answer.

He had to get down and crawl, the wet dirt caking on his hands and knees. He poked his head up through the vines to look around and the moon fought through thin clouds and silhouetted the hillside. He ducked down again and kept crawling, pushing between the bushes and weeds and remembering the machete he left behind. Feeling the rise of the valley and when he poked his head up through the vines again he saw the two white dots of the headlights. Their beams shining on the shed in the backyard of Celia's house. He was then able to climb up from beneath and step over and across the vines, his knees rising high and his arms held wide for balance as he navigated his way up the hillside. Cuts and scratches across his arms and neck and bleeding now.

He fought his way out of the kudzu. Bent over with his hands on his knees and caught his breath. Gripping the dress. And then he rose back up and walked into the shine of the headlights. Covered in dirty trails of sweat and blood. His lank hair stuck against his head and neck and a red welt across his forehead. Colburn waited there for someone to move or to say something and he wanted it to be a friend or at least someone he could reach out to and say I have to go find that boy right now and come with me. Come help me. He wanted this though he knew no such thing existed. He was alone. He moved closer to the front of the truck and a voice called for him to stop right there. And then the door opened. He raised his arm to shield the light and he was about to call out to the dark figure that had moved around to the side of the hood when he saw the steel shadow of the shotgun barrel.

'Where is she?' Dixon said.

Colburn lowered his hands and took a step toward Dixon but Dixon shoved the barrel toward him and said don't you fucking move.

'What's in your hand?'

'It's not what you think,' Colburn said.

'Show it to me.'

'Shit, Dixon. Get the hell out of the way.'

'Show it.'

Dixon raised the shotgun and lined the barrel with Colburn's forehead. The headlights shined across the valley, the two beams the only thing separating the two men and bugs danced in the light and the engine hummed. Colburn let the dress fall from his fist and it dangled from the straps wrapped around his index finger.

The barrel began to wobble as Dixon's hands began to tremble.

'It's not what you think,' Colburn said.

'It's exactly what I think.'

Dixon shook. He choked down grunts of heartbreak.

'Get down,' Dixon said.

'You need to listen to me.'

'Get down.'

'I found the dress and I know where it came from. You gotta take me to Myer.'

'Shut up,' he said. His voice shaking like his hands and not the vision of strength and power he wanted to be but instead crumbling.

'You have a wife,' Colburn said.

'Don't you tell me nothing.'

'Think about her.'

'I said shut your goddamn mouth,' Dixon said. The barrel rose and the blast came with a white-hot flash as Dixon fired over Colburn's head. The shot echoed across the valley, a tumble of sound that didn't seem to stop. Colburn threw his hands over his head and cowered, then dropped down to his knees and tried to shrink into the earth and with his eyes closed and ears ringing the boot heel smashed against his forehead, mashing the already tender bruise from where the shovel had smacked him. He fell to his side, writhing in pain as Dixon stood over him and Colburn could not wait any longer and he said it was the boy. The boy with the shopping cart that you see all over town. He had the dress and he's got other shit of mine and hers out there in that house. I swear to God I just came from out there and I'll show you. Jesus I'll show you just don't shoot again. I swear to God. Colburn propped himself with one arm and raised his hand to Dixon and said please.

'Get up and get in before I kill you,' Dixon said. 'I don't know what the hell you did but I could kill you right now and wouldn't nobody give a damn. Not one damn soul.'

Colburn reached out and grabbed the truck bumper and pulled himself to his feet. He moved for the passenger side but Dixon said hold on. You're driving and if you move one muscle the wrong way I'll shoot your ass. He then motioned with the shotgun barrel toward the driver's seat and Colburn passed through the headlights and then sat down behind the wheel. Before Dixon could make it around to the other side Colburn shifted into drive and stomped the gas. The truck wheels spinning and spinning in the wet ground and Dixon panicked, jumping back with a quick little dance and getting his finger on the trigger as the truck fishtailed forward. Dixon raised the barrel and yelled and Colburn eased off the gas just enough for the tires to gain traction and then came the blast and the back window shattered. The glass exploded all around Colburn as he ducked down but kept his foot on the gas. Raising his head again just in time to dodge a pecan tree and then making it onto the gravel. Another blast across the night that found no home as Colburn slid onto the road and raced toward town.

He stopped at the pay phone outside the gas station and he dialed zero. Asked to be connected to the sheriff. Yes, it's a motherfucking emergency. Myer was pacing in his living room when the phone rang and ten minutes later he pulled into the gas station and found Colburn sitting on the tailgate of Dixon's truck like some sullied mannequin. Celia's dress draped across his lap.

56

THE BOY WAS PICKED UP the next morning as he pushed the shopping cart along the side of the road. He had stopped to lean on a fencepost and watch a calf following around its mother when the cruiser came along and parked itself in the middle of the road. Myer and his deputy put the boy into the backseat and left the shopping cart there like some roadside relic that would one day provide an explanation of this moment for curious passersby.

The boy sat in a square room at a square table and Myer soon discovered practically nothing. The boy wasn't certain how old he was. He wasn't sure of his name or the names of the man and the woman. He had never been to school. He did not know the name of the town he was in now or the names of any of the other places he claimed to have wandered about with the man and woman. He did not know the month or the year and he could not read or write. He made intimation that there had once been a little boy with them but he did not know his name either or what exactly happened to him.

He told them about the hole and tried to tell them about the man but he could not explain himself in a way that satisfied. He talked about the woman. Myer asked him what woman? The woman that was with you before or Celia? He nodded. And then he shook his head. And then he only said that woman. That one. He mentioned her screaming as if he had been there when it came out of her mouth and not off in the distance. His explanations confusing to both Myer and the men in ties that sat in chairs behind the boy. Their arms folded. Their minds made up as the boy admitted having the dress. Admitted knowing where she was. The broken chronology of how he found the hole and went down inside and what happened to either the woman or Celia or both. He spoke in rudimentary fragments that sometimes made sense and sometimes didn't. A mixture of subjects and hand motions. He could not explain the man. His blood-red and vacant eyes and his fidgets and how the man had become something worse than he had been before. He didn't know how to explain it or name it. All he could muster was he went down in there after.

'After?' Myer asked. 'What was he down in there after?'

'He was after them others,' the boy said.

'What do you mean? What others?'

'He was after.'

'After what? You put him in this hole after you put the others in the hole?'

'Naw.'

'Then you put him in before the others?'

The questions looped and spun and he finally would not answer, sinking down into the chair. His eyes lowering and rubbing at his own skinny arms and his head moving in little spasms.

Go on and tell us about it, they said. Pushing him. Tell us exactly like you know it. You used to go in the bar and eat with Celia. She liked you, didn't she? Did you like her? She sure was nice to you, sounds like. Go on and tell us. Who did you put down in that hole?

But he wouldn't talk anymore. His cheeks and eyes working in twitches of frustration and he shifted in the chair as if in pain. Myer told him to calm down and they gave him a glass of water and then left him alone in the room. Watched through the door window as if he were some sideshow with his own language. His own manner of surviving. His own rules that they believed could only be savage and this dark place that he spoke of down in the valley. This creature. Though he had long been born and alive and moving among them it was only now that he seemed to be part of the workings of men.

The boy was held for two days. During that time Colburn took Myer and the investigators to the buried house, a house the search party had gone into when the twins disappeared but which was now decorated with stick figures and keepsakes of the vanished. He took them to the spring where Celia's shoes were still waiting. He stood with them in the bar and explained how she fed the boy and treated the boy. He told Myer everything about the argument with Dixon and what Dixon had said about Colburn's father and Celia's mother and how it had set him off. How he went out to Celia's house and lost it and tore up shit. How he looked for Celia at the spring and she was gone and how he waited for her to show up but she didn't. How he remembered what she had told him about the house down there and it felt like a message and that made him go look.

The boy ate everything they gave him and they made him take a shower and dressed him in an orange jumpsuit that was big and floppy on his wiry frame. They gave him socks and tennis shoes that fit. Colburn came to see him once. He sat with the boy in the cell and Myer had given him questions to ask, only in a more gentle tone. In a stripped-down language that he hoped the boy would understand. Colburn talked about Celia and said I know she was good. She was good to you. We all liked her. He asked where he had been when she went down to the spring. He asked about the man and woman. He asked about the twins. But the boy only stared at him. The only question he would answer was when Colburn was on his way out and he turned and asked the boy why he hit him with the shovel when he was in the house and the boy looked up with worried eyes and said I figured you was him come back.

On the morning of the third day they loaded the boy in the cruiser and drove out to the valley and told him show us where they are. The boy led Myer and the two investigators to the cave. The smell had strengthened and filled the length of the tunnel and rose from the entrance. This the hole you've been talking about? one of the men asked. The boy nodded and the men climbed down. Covered their mouths and turned on their flashlights and followed the boy deep inside. All the way to the pit.

The three men shined their lights down into the black. Amazed by its depth. Sickened by the smell. Beginning to try and figure out what all they were going to need to get in there and find out how far down they would have to go. The spots of light danced around in the dark as they studied the tunnel and on the other side of the pit the boy spotted a rope-like root hanging from the distant edge. Myer and the investigators exchanged sentiments of disbelief. About the cave and the tunnel. About the real live shit that people here aren't going to want to believe. While they talked the boy reached down and rolled up the pantlegs of the jumpsuit, getting them off his feet and rolling them to his thighs. Then he retied his shoes.

He darted right between them and dove out into the dark, flying across the pit with open and hopeful hands.

'Jesus,' Myer yelled. Their flashlight beams chased him and the boy had caught hold of the end of the root with one hand, his body floating over nothing.

'Holy damn shit,' another man said.

The boy swung back and forth. They all waited for the root to tear free and for the boy to disappear. But the root held. The boy was making a long and irritated wail like a siren as he reached his other hand up and took hold. And little by little he inched his way up.

Myer drew his pistol from the holster. They held their lights on him and watched the struggle. His twisting torso as he grunted and sweated. A trail of blood down the side of one hand and running down his arm.

'He ain't gonna make it anyway,' one of them said. The boy kicked and jerked. Pulled and grunted and he steadily pulled himself up the root. And he made it. Climbing until he reached his hand above earth and grabbing hold of a thick cut of rock. Getting his leg thrown up onto the side. And then rising out of the pit and falling flat on his back. Exhausted and heaving but alive.

'Get your ass back over here,' one of them said.

'Don't go no further,' Myer said.

The boy stood. The pantlegs had come loose in his struggle and covered his legs and feet. He rolled them up again. Looked at the blood on his hands. The three beams in his face and their voices throwing hard warnings across the pit. Warnings that echoed and then disappeared.

'Shoot him,' one of them said.

'For what?' Myer said.

'He's running off.'

'Don't move,' Myer said.

'What are you gonna tell these people if you let him get away?'

The boy brushed himself off and then he turned and began to move further into the tunnel. Their lights moving around in frustration and their shouts and the argument between them. Shoot him. I'm not shooting him. You'd better goddamn shoot him. I said no. The boy moved deeper and deeper. His figure disappearing from the light. A vision of the underworld slipping away and then as he faded into black, the pistol fired once. And then twice more.

57

A ROAD HAD BEEN CUT and cleared leading down to the cave and the tunnel, and there pulleys and ropes were used to lower men down into the pit and bring up the bodies of the woman and the man, the twins, and Celia. Dixon had been onsite during the creation of the road and the digging down to the tunnel and the pit, overseeing the equipment. Making sure it was handled right. And he had been standing there when they raised Celia from the pit and once her body was laid on the ground, he had turned and walked out of the valley. He drove to his office and turned in his keys to the secretary and then he drove home and turned in his house key to Sadie. After the job of digging out the bodies was finished the bulldozers and excavators were left there. Waiting for the dead season. Readied for attack.

During the interim months of autumn Myer replayed every step he had taken since the moment he met the man and the woman and the boy hanging around their broke-down Cadillac in the post office parking lot. Sometimes he cussed himself for not towing their car to the garage and paying whatever it took to get it running and then telling the man to get behind the wheel and follow him. Driving to the county line while he watched in his rearview mirror to make sure they were not slipping off down some backroad and then stopping at the line and giving them fifty dollars and a bag of sandwiches and telling them to keep going and don't come back. Other times he cussed himself for ignoring them. You saw that boy and that woman walking back and forth to town. You saw what they were doing. Looking through the garbage. Hanging around in the alley behind the café waiting for scraps. You knew that man was shit but you could have given that boy some work and given that woman some work because she said they looked for it. You saw them and you let them be and you knew something was not right. But you did nothing. You watched. He cussed himself for not pushing them away and he cussed himself for not reaching out and both sides of introspection caused equal bouts of regret that kept him walking around his pond at night with the moon reflecting on the still water like some pale and all-knowing eye.

Winter came. The kudzu leaves died with the cold, leaving the valley covered in a mangled netting of brown and gray vines. A leafless netting that exposed the plants and trees and ground below, the beaten and buried land gaining the light of a December sun. The work began and went on for months. The vines and the undergrowth ripped from the earth. The decrepit house leveled. The trees cut to stumps and then the stumps wrapped in chains and pulled up and across the valley lay massive piles of trees and brush and wadded vines. Piles that were then burned, the smoke clouds hanging across the valley and hanging over the town like great and mindful spirits and at night the fires burned in high reaching blazes of red and gold. The surviving roots of the kudzu vines hid deep in the ground where man could not see and not know and one day they would return. Moving in increments. Time no obstacle. Waiting patiently for their sins to be forgotten.

58

THE BOY WAS NEVER FOUND. Colburn heard the townspeople talking about him.

They called the boy a murderer. A devil worshiper. A killer.
A butcher. He heard them when he was in the hardware
store and he heard them huddled on the sidewalks. Colburn
moved about town and rarely spoke and kept his eyes away
from theirs and he began to imagine the boy on the streets
again. Pushing the shopping cart. Looking into garbage cans.
Being told to go away. Meandering toward the bar in hopes
of a moment of respite. Hoping to eat. And as time went on
he saw the boy more often and he noticed him more closely
now. His bent neck and the rough skin of his cheeks and the
way his eyes seemed to hide beneath his brow. He saw the
boy in the day and he saw the boy in the twilight as he stood
and looked across the war-torn valley and soon he realized
the gravity of his own judgment.

He wanted to tell the boy I know it wasn't you. I don't know
what it was but I know it wasn't you and it's not your fault. He
said it into the wind as he drove around in the flatbed truck.
He said it as he sat in the dented aluminum chair in Celia's
backyard in the middle of star-struck nights, hoping for her
to come and haunt him. He said it to the boy and then he
said it to himself. It's not your fault. Thinking of his own life

as a boy. What if someone had said that to me. It's not your fault. He thought of the boy and the life he had lived and the way he looked and his inability to participate and all that he had missed and would forever miss. It's not your fault and I looked at you the same way the world looked at you and I should have known better. But it was too late now and one solitary evening as he stood and watched the final light bleed across the bare hillsides he said to the boy you are my brother in this world. And I wish I would have known it.

He spent his last days in Red Bluff sitting on Celia's porch. Still somehow waiting to see her again. Imagining her sitting there with him, drinking from the bottle. The flecks of polish on her toenails. Her aura of peace and care. Go away, he heard himself say to her with his hands swollen and bleeding from his rampage. She came to you and you told her to go away and she did. The one goddamn thing you asked for that you got. He picked up a cigarette butt from the ashtray that sat on a stack of magazines. The end with pink from her lipstick. He tucked it in his pocket and took one more look at the big electric hand in the window before walking out between the pecan trees and getting in the flatbed and driving away. Leaving all of his tools and scrap in the building downtown.

He found work on the Mississippi River boats that took him away for weeks at a time. On the days in between he lived a solitary existence in the motels of river towns and decades came and went. When he realized he was sick he did not go to a doctor and he did not try and treat himself. He allowed it to come. An aching in his bones and his strength diminishing and a shortness of breath. His hands shaking and lying in bed except to go to the bathroom or to try and eat something and in the last weeks of his life the voices from the valley found him and in his fevered delusion he was no longer alone in a motel room but in a house where children roamed freely.

In his worst moments of pain he would scream at the world that he believed had failed him so badly and that was when an old woman appeared in the house with her frazzled gray hair and crusted blood in her nose and a cackle that fell somewhere between laughing and crying. The children would then disappear as if frightened by the demented old woman who came to visit the sick man, but one child returned again in moments of appeasement and exhaustion when she left him alone. The child would sit on the edge of the bed and talk to Colburn in a serenity of brotherhood he had never known. And the child would make promises. Suggestions of being together in a future unbound. Colburn had read through stiff motel room Bibles and sometime he found comfort in the passages and other times he realized how far short he had fallen and he felt the hellfire that had been set forth for him by his mother and father from the moment of conception. A damned child born into a damned world where there was nothing to do but accept the rejection waiting for him. In those last days he feared the uncertainty of what lay ahead but he believed it was going to hurt. Because he had raged against the life given to him and had never tried anything different. He had cursed bitterly against his mother and father. Against the force that robbed him of Celia. Against the valley that wanted more and took it. Against his own guilt for the anger that sent her down the pathway. Inside him a bitterness had grown and spread through his body and warmed his blood and now blended with the sickness that coursed through his veins.

In his final bedridden and delirious days he cried out for

the child to come and stay with him and when the child returned, the child begged him to say it. All you have to do is say it. But he would not. He wanted the world to beg him for forgiveness and not the other way around. Say it, the child would tell him. Say it and we can go away together. You can be my brother.

No.

In the last hours of his life they argued and argued some more and then he felt himself relinquish. And lighten. As if a multitude of tender hands touched his body and lifted him. He felt himself above. Outside and down the river and then across the valley of kudzu. Looking down into the force of nature. Say it, the child whispered. It's not your fault. The hands held him and carried him to the space between light and dark and then he said it. I'm sorry. He felt his spirit lift and he felt the weight of sickness and solitude disappear and he said it again and again. I'm sorry. And the multitude of hands held him between the light and the dark and then they let him go. Waiting to see if his spirit would rise. Or if it would fall.

Acknowledgments

My thanks go to Josh Kendall, Reagan Arthur, Ellen Levine, Yuli Masinovsky, Jason Richman, Ion Mills, and Geoffrey Mulligan. I also want to thank Sabrea, Presley, and Brooklyn, the crew that keeps me truckin'.

NO EXIT PRESS

More than just the usual suspects

— CWA DAGGER —
BEST CRIME & MYSTERY
PUBLISHER 2019

'A very smart, independent publisher delivering
the finest literary crime fiction' – *Big Issue*

MEET NO EXIT PRESS, the independent publisher bringing you the best in crime and noir fiction. From classic detective novels, to page-turning spy thrillers and singular writing that just grabs the attention. Our books are carefully crafted by some of the world's finest writers and delivered to you by a small, but mighty, team.

In our 30 years of business, we have published award-winning fiction and non-fiction including the work of a Pulitzer Prize winner, the British Crime Book of the Year, numerous CWA Dagger Awards, a British million copy bestselling author, the winner of the Canadian Governor General's Award for Fiction and the Scotiabank Giller Prize, to name but a few. We are the home of many crime and noir legends from the USA whose work includes iconic film adaptations and TV sensations. We pride ourselves in uncovering the most exciting new or undiscovered talents. New and not so new – you know who you are!!

We are a proactive team committed to delivering the very best, both for our authors and our readers.

Want to join the conversation and find out more about what we do?

Catch us on social media or sign up to our newsletter for all the latest news from No Exit Press HQ.

f fb.me/noexitpress **𝕐** @noexitpress
noexit.co.uk/newsletter